THE GIANT WHIRLED . . .

. . . and swung a Bowie from somewhere inside his coat in a sweeping arc toward Slocum's face.

Slocum took a half step back, just beyond the reach of the deadly blade. He blocked its passage with his forearm, catching his assailant's lightning move with his wrist.

At the same instant, Slocum fired point-blank into the man's chest . . .

**DON'T MISS THESE
ALL-ACTION WESTERN SERIES
FROM THE BERKLEY PUBLISHING GROUP**

THE GUNSMITH by J. R. Roberts
Clint Adams was a legend among lawmen, outlaws, and ladies.
They called him . . . the Gunsmith.

LONGARM by Tabor Evans
The popular long-running series about U.S. Deputy Marshal
Long—his life, his loves, his fight for justice.

SLOCUM by Jake Logan
Today's longest-running action Western. John Slocum rides a
deadly trail of hot blood and cold steel.

BUSHWHACKERS by B. J. Lanagan
An action-packed series by the creators of Longarm! The rousing
adventures of the most brutal gang of cutthroats ever assembled—
Quantrill's Raiders.

JAKE LOGAN

SLOCUM AND THE COMANCHE PRINCESS

JOVE BOOKS, NEW YORK

SLOCUM AND THE COMANCHE PRINCESS

A Jove Book / published by arrangement with
the author

PRINTING HISTORY
Jove edition / February 1999

All rights reserved.
Copyright © 1999 by Jove Publications, Inc.
This book may not be reproduced in whole or in part,
by mimeograph or any other means, without permission.
For information address: The Berkley Publishing Group,
a member of Penguin Putnam Inc.,
375 Hudson Street, New York, New York 10014.

The Penguin Putnam Inc. World Wide Web site address is
http://www.penguinputnam.com

ISBN: 0-515-12449-4

A JOVE BOOK®
Jove Books are published by The Berkley Publishing Group,
a member of Penguin Putnam Inc.,
375 Hudson Street, New York, New York 10014.
JOVE and the "J" design
are trademarks belonging to Jove Publications, Inc.

PRINTED IN THE UNITED STATES OF AMERICA

10 9 8 7 6 5 4 3 2 1

SLOCUM AND THE
COMANCHE PRINCESS

1

When Slocum saw her for the first time, he was on his way to Fort Sill in the company of a cavalry patrol under the command of one still too young to realize the dangers. With forty troopers moving in a slow column behind him, Captain Boyd Carter had no idea that the men riding a string of wiry little ponies across the hilltop in front of them were the most feared of all Plains tribes, the Kwahadie Comanche. John Slocum recognized them at once by the single braid of black hair hanging down their backs and the pair of eagle feathers tied to fall carelessly across their shoulders.

"Indians!" Captain Carter exclaimed, reaching clumsily for his pistol and jerking his horse to a halt.

"I wouldn't do that if I were you, Cap'n," Slocum warned as the Indians rode slowly down the grassy slope toward the cavalry patrol. "Those aren't just Indians. They're Kwahadies. I'm sure they don't mean us any harm or we'd already be in the fight of our lives. They're lettin' us see them, so they don't want trouble."

"What the hell is a Kwahadie?" Carter asked tersely. He sounded angry, but he left his gun in its holster.

Slocum sat his horse with his hands resting in plain sight on his saddlehorn, making it clear to the Indians he had peaceful intentions. "A Kwahadie is a Comanche, Cap'n, the worst of the five bands when it comes to fighting and torture, but by the look of 'em we're in luck today. This isn't a war party. They've got a few women with 'em." He noticed one girl in particular. She wore a deerskin dress, and the fringed bottom of her skirt was riding high on her slender, slightly muscular legs, which were clamped to the pony's sides. Her long black hair framed an oval face with broad cheekbones. She rode with four other woman behind the Comanche men.

"If they're Comanches, they're off the reservation illegally, Mr. Slocum, and my orders are to see to it that all Comanche and Kiowa Indians remain inside the boundaries. I intend to tell them so . . . at gunpoint, if necessary."

"Aiming a gun at this bunch would be a mistake," Slocum said as his eyes swept the hills, making a quick count of the warriors. "We're badly outnumbered, and the Kwahadie men are carrying rifles. Your soldiers won't stand a chance against them. You told me on the way up from Childress your men are raw recruits. Soldiers who don't know how to fight Comanches won't last very long. If it was up to me, I'd see what they want before I started a fight we can't win."

"You appear to have too much respect for these heathens, Mr. Slocum. They are nothing more than half-naked savages with a few single-shot rifles. We have repeaters, the latest Winchester issue."

"Your boys won't hardly get the chance to use 'em," Slocum said, wishing he'd ridden alone into Indian Territory instead of seeking a bit of company in this empty land. The company he had so eagerly sought was on the verge of getting him killed if Captain Carter ordered his men to draw their rifles. Unless you had fought against the Kwahadies, it was hard to understand why this particular tribe had such a menacing reputation. "They may be half naked, like you say, and their guns may not be as good as the ones your men are carrying. But I promise you they'll kill every man in your company before it's over if you give the order to fire. I'm no coward, but I'm sure as hell not gonna hang around to see how it comes out. I'm bettin' this Palouse stud of mine can outrun those ponies. I damn sure ain't gonna help you fight Kwahadies. If you're foolish enough to try it, you'll do it on your own."

Carter gave him a cold stare. "Are you calling me a fool?" he asked.

"Only if you start shooting at these Indians, Cap'n. Then I'm gonna call you worse than a fool, only you won't hear me say it because you'll be lying somewhere in all this grass with your belly slit open, your eyelids cut off so your eyeballs will boil in the sun, and your scalp tied to the stock of one of those old rifles. You'll still be alive for a few hours, but you won't hear much besides your own screaming. I've heard of a few men the Kwahadies sliced up who lived for two, three days."

Carter, a pink-faced youth of twenty-five or so with close-cropped red hair, gave the Indians a closer look. "I suppose we can find out what they want before I order them back to the reservation."

"There's another mistake you're making," Slocum said, with his eye on the woman. "Kwahadies don't follow orders. If I was you, I'd ask 'em real nice to go back where they belong, unless they've got a good reason for being here."

"This is army business, Mr. Slocum," Carter snapped. "I won't let a civilian tell me how to do my job."

Slocum shrugged. "I was only trying to keep you and your men alive, Cap'n. But if you're of a mind to die today, then by all means give those Kwahadies a good dose of army business. I won't be here to see to burying you and your troopers. Forty graves is too much digging for a man who ain't inclined to use a shovel in the first place. Let the buzzards pick your bones. Tonight the coyotes and wolves will clean up what's left, and by tomorrow there won't hardly be any sign of what happened here. Maybe a few bloodstains on the grass.''

The young captain swallowed, still watching the Indians as he too counted them. "There are only forty or so," he said, but with less conviction now. "With repeating rifles, I say we stand a good chance of defeating them. I won't take any guff off of a savage, no matter what variety they may be. If they won't go back to the reservation peacefully, I'll order my men to draw and shoot to kill."

Despite the seriousness of their situation, Slocum chuckled softly. "You may get that order out of your mouth, but getting it accomplished is gonna be a little tougher. Before your men can get their rifles out, half of 'em will have bullet holes in their fancy new uniforms. The other half will last a little longer . . . maybe long enough to fire one shot before the Kwahadies cut them down. Of course, like I told you, I won't be here to see it. I'll hear it from a distance, from the other side of those hills yonder, 'cause I'm gonna ask this stud for all the speed he's got. Like you told me just now, this is army business and I ain't a soldier. No sense in me hanging around to get killed if it's none of my business."

A thick-chested warrior riding at the front of the Indians gave the sign for peace. Captain Carter sat motionless with a puzzled look on his face.

"He gave you the sign for peace, Cap'n," Slocum said.

"I don't understand Indian sign language. I'll speak to him instead."

"He won't understand English."

"Then how shall I tell him to ride back to the reservation?"

"I don't reckon you will, not in words they understand. If you want, and if you'll promise there won't be any shooting, I'll translate for you."

"Do you speak Comanche, Mr. Slocum?"

"Some. Sign language is universal among Plains tribes. It's how they communicate with other tribes when they don't speak the same tongue. I'll have to use a little of both," he said as the Comanches rode closer, within a hundred yards of the front of the column.

Slocum gave the sign for peace and then the sign for "I speak true words." Then his gaze wandered to the girl again. A beaded necklace hung between the swells of her large breasts. They strained the front of her dress, and her hard nipples made tiny peaks where they swayed back and forth with the gait of her gray pony mare.

The Comanches halted, spreading out to form a ragged line that blocked the soldiers' path. Then their leader began using more sign talk, watching Slocum carefully each time he made another series of movements with his hands.

"He says his people are hungry, Cap'n. The meat they gave 'em at Fort Sill had worms in it, and it made the children sick. They decided to go hunting for deer or the last of the buffalo, the ones white hide hunters haven't killed. He says the women and children are starving. They have nothing to eat."

Carter turned to Slocum. "The meat rations had worms?" he asked.

"That's what he told me, and he signed for true words. You're new out here, Cap'n Carter. You and your green troopers are about to find out just how bad the army treats reservation Indians. It's enough to make you sick. The older ones starve themselves so the children can eat because the Indian agent won't give them enough food for everybody. The old people make this sacrifice so the children won't die."

"I don't believe it," Carter said, but he could see that the rib bones were showing on most of the warriors. "They do look a little on the skinny side, however."

Slocum took a deep breath, casting another glance at the beautiful Comanche maiden. "If you want my advice, and if you have any compassion for starving kids and women, you'll let 'em hunt for whatever they can find. Nearly all the buffalo are gone these days, but Kwahadies are good hunters. They'll find a few deer and go back to the reservation with the meat so their people won't starve.''

"Colonel Dudley wired us our orders when we got off the train in Fort Worth, that if we ran into any Indians on the way up to Fort Sill, we should order them back or kill them.''

Slocum heard less conviction in Carter's voice now. "You're the one who has to live with your conscience, Cap'n. When you see conditions at Fort Sill, you'll understand. A bunch of crooks got the beef contracts at the fort. I've been there half a dozen times and I've seen it before. Most of the beef is too rotten to eat, and what flour they get is moldy. It's a damn shame to treat human beings the way these people are treated, and once you see it for yourself, you'll be glad you didn't start a fight with this bunch. Let 'em go. All they're doing is what any man would do if his children were hungry.''

"I suppose you're right," Carter replied, chewing his lower lip. "You can tell them about those two old buffalo bulls we saw back at the river. I won't order them back to the reservation after what you've told me, only I want you to ask them to give me their word they'll come back when they've found something to eat.''

Slocum began giving sign talk to the Comanche leader, every now and then sneaking a quick look at the girl. She was staring at him. He thought he could see the hint of a smile on her face.

When he'd done the best he could to convey Captain Carter's message, he signed for an end to their talk.

The Comanche closed his fist over his heart.

"He's saying thanks, that he is glad you have a pure heart so his people won't die of hunger." As Slocum spoke, his eyes wandered briefly to the young woman.

"Did they promise to go back to the reservation?" Carter asked.

Slocum knew the Indians would go back on their own, but to satisfy the captain he said, "They sure did.''

Suddenly the Comanche leader gave Slocum several quick motions with his hands, inclining his head toward the girl.

Slocum signed that he understood. He had just been warned that the girl was the daughter of a Kwahadie chief and she was another man's property.

"Suvate," he said, a Comanche word with several meanings, including an agreement that it was over, the way he was looking at the girl, yet Slocum found himself wishing for a way to get to know her, to speak with her alone. She was one of the most beautiful, shapely Indian maidens he'd ever seen, and his lustful side was struggling with his better judgment.

"Column forward!" Captain Carter cried, signaling his men to move on.

Slocum forced his eyes away from the girl and heeled his Palouse forward.

2

The little town of Cache in Indian Territory was close to Fort Sill. It was a city of tents and clapboard buildings, saloons and whorehouses, gambling establishments and general mercantiles. Slocum left the company of Captain Carter and his troops as soon as the fort was in sight, silently thankful that there had been no run-in with the Kwahadie Comanches. Army officers like Carter were a part of the problem in what was sometimes called the Indian Nations north of the Red River, and when green soldiers were combined with dishonest Indian agents it created even more ill feeling between red men and white. Beef was the prime commodity. Various Indian tribes—the Comanche bands, the Kiowa, and the Arapaho—were crowded together on barren land like caged animals. For nomadic people, staying in one place was punishment enough. But to be fed spoiled food by the so-called Great White Father in Washington was an even larger disgrace, causing unrest among the more warlike tribes.

Slocum reined his stud to a halt in front of a saloon at midday. He craved good whiskey, but he was certain that it couldn't be found in a place like Cache, where pure corn squeezings were flavored with tobacco juice and ginger and colored to resemble the good stuff from Kentucky and Tennessee. A late fall wind swept down Cache's Main Street, sweeping fallen leaves of every color and shape into swirling clouds. He tied off the Palouse and climbed onto a porch of sagging planks. Despite the chill in the air, he opened his coat so he could get at his Colt .44 if the need arose.

Pushing through a pair of batwing doors, he found the place empty of patrons. A sign above the false-fronted building read THE WAGON WHEEL, and by all appearances the wheel had stopped turning right at that moment.

A stocky bartender eyed the gun in his cross-pull holster. "We don't allow no firearms in here," he said. "You have to check that pistol with me till you're ready to leave."

Slocum carried a .32-caliber bellygun inside his shirt, but the notion of being without his Colt didn't sit well. "I'm only interested in buying a bottle of your best whiskey. Then I'll leave to find a room for the night."

A woman with flaming red hair emerged from a door behind the bar while Slocum was speaking, distracting his attention from the barkeep. She wore a low-cut green velvet dress that revealed the tops of her milky breasts. Her pretty face was lightly freckled. She smiled when she saw Slocum.

"Don't matter I don't reckon," the barman said, "seein' as we ain't busy." He noticed Slocum staring at the girl. "This here's Fannie. You can keep your gun fer now. A shot of our best is two bits a glass."

"How good is your best?" Slocum inquired without taking his eyes off Fannie's ample bosom.

"Tolerable. Indian Territory ain't exactly the place to find honest whiskey, mister. Cowboys an' soldiers can't tell the difference when they're thirsty. But I've got a bottle of French brandy hid under the bar, if brandy's more to your likin'."

"The brandy sounds good. How about if I buy Miss Fannie a glass?"

Fannie nodded, smiling. "I'd be happy to share a glass

of brandy with you, stranger,'' she said, coming around the bar to reveal more of her figure. She had a tiny waist and the hourglass swell of her hips was mighty inviting to a man who'd been on the trail for six lonely days.

"Pick a table," Fannie said, sweeping a hand around the empty room.

"This one'll do," he told her, drawing back a chair for her. "My name's John Slocum, so we'll be properly acquainted."

"Pleased to meet you, Mr. Slocum." She took the chair he offered her, arranging the split in her skirt to show off the bulge of her thigh where a silk stocking met her garter belt.

He took a seat beside her while the bartender poured their drinks. "You're a pretty girl, Fannie. That brandy is gonna taste a lot better keepin' company with you."

"You say the nicest things, Mr. Slocum. If I'm not being too forward, you're a downright handsome man. Taller than most men I meet."

"I was fed real good when I was a kid so I'd grow."

She giggled, then her eyes strayed to his crotch for a moment. "Are you a married man?" she asked, fluttering her long eyelashes. Her eyes were a dark green that matched her velvet dress.

"I'm not good material for a husband. Never even tried my hand at being married."

"Oh? Why do you say you aren't good husband material?"

"I move around quite a bit. A woman wants a man who stays at home real regular. That just never was my style. Maybe I haven't met the right woman yet."

"It sounds to me like you aren't really looking," she said as their drinks arrived.

Slocum tossed a silver dollar on the table. The barman swept it into his palm and left. "I'm keeping an eye open for just the right one. I'm partial to redheads, only I've been told they have a bad temper."

She smiled again. "That isn't true. I'm good-natured and very passionate with the type of man I prefer."

"What type is that?" he asked, pleased by the direction their conversation was taking.

"Tall men with black hair. Men like you," she replied, taking a sip of brandy. "I have a few other requirements."

"And what might those requirements be?" he asked, playing into her hands.

"I like men who are rough, but rough in a gentle way, if you know what I mean."

"I think I understand," he told her. He tasted his drink and found it to his liking. "You want a man who treats you like a lady until bedtime."

"That's a very brash way of putting it, Mr. Slocum."

"I hope I'm not being too bold. If so, you have my apology. I can see you're a real lady. I'm betting it's only some misfortune that forced you to work in a saloon."

"How true," she said thoughtfully. "I've had more than my share of misfortune. As soon as I get together enough money, I'm blowing this hayseed town. Cache isn't what I'd call much of a town anyway. I hate this place."

"How did you come to be stranded here?" he asked with as much sympathy in his voice as he could muster.

"It's a long story. A gentleman friend and me were headed out to California. He was a gambler. And a heavy drinker. One night a few months ago, he lost all our money and took off with another woman. She had money, so I was told. He left me here to fend for myself. He was a rotten bastard, if you'll pardon my unladylike language."

"Perfectly understandable, under the circumstances. I don't know anything about your gentleman friend, but it sounds to me like he was no kind of gentleman at all."

"He wasn't. Clyde was a no-good bastard for doing me this way. I hope he gets what he deserves one of these days. I hope she leaves him."

Slocum sensed the nearness of a chance to bed Fannie. An angry woman, one who was angry at a man, was easy pickings. "If you care to dine with me later on, I'll buy you the best meal Cache has to offer."

She looked him up and down, toying with her glass. "I just may accept your invitation, Mr. Slocum. Let me think on it some. The best place in town is down the street. It's called the Palace. I can't usually afford to go there. The Wagon Wheel doesn't exactly have the best clientele. Soldiers don't spend much money. I make a dollar or two in tips on busy nights, and Oliver pays me two dollars a day to serve the drinks. My room at the boardinghouse is hardly bigger than a closet, but it's all I can afford right now. I'm saving all I can to get out of this lousy town. Stagecoach to Santa Fe costs almost twenty dollars. Then I'm going to work somewhere until I can save enough to get to San Francisco. I've heard it's the most beautiful city in the world."

"I like San Francisco, only it's too crowded for me. I like quieter places usually."

"You've been to San Francisco? Oh, Mr. Slocum! Please tell me all about it—the opera houses and big hotels, the fancy dress shops. I want to hear all about it."

"Maybe I can describe it to you over dinner at the Palace tonight," he suggested.

"I accept. I can't wait to hear about San Francisco. I'll tell Oliver I'm going home early this evening. I'll change into my best dress . . . the only nice dress I have. I must confess I'm excited."

Slocum felt excited looking at the high bulge of her breasts above her corset. "It would be my pleasure. Where should I call for you?"

Her smile fell into a frown. "I'll have to meet you there. Miz Williams won't allow single women at the boarding house to have gentleman callers."

"I'll meet you at the Palace at eight," he agreed. "I noticed there's only one hotel in Cache. I'll get a room there and put my horse in the stable. I hope they have a bathhouse. Last time I had a real bath and a shave was back in Fort Worth.''

"I'm afraid the Grand Hotel isn't very grand, Mr. Slocum, but the rooms aren't all that bad. Ask for a room upstairs if they have one, which I'm sure they will. It's a slow time of year for a frontier town. The cattle drives have already been through on their way to the Kansas railheads.''

"I'll ask for an upstairs room.'' He downed his brandy and signaled for another.

Again her gaze strayed to his crotch. He watched her out of the corner of his eye. He wondered what Fannie would be like in bed. His years of experience with women convinced him he would have his way with her tonight, if he went about it carefully. All day his mind had been on the beautiful Comanche maiden he saw with the Kwahadie hunting party. But with Fannie as a distraction, he soon forgot about the Indian girl.

"Where are you headed, Mr. Slocum?'' she asked. "If I'm not being too nosy.''

"Not at all. I'm riding back to Denver, though I've given some thought to passing through Santa Fe first to see about a few good mares. I'm in the horse business from time to time. Good blooded stock.'' He dangled the possibility of a side trip to Santa Fe as bait. Later tonight, she would ask him if she could accompany him. He was sure of it. Fannie wanted out of Cache. Having been a traveling gambler's woman, she wouldn't be coy or retiring when it came to getting what she wanted.

Her renewed smile showed him how right he was. "Santa Fe?! I've been dreaming of Santa Fe for months. I just know I could find work there. Then I could make enough money to get to San Francisco.''

"Santa Fe is a busy place,'' he agreed. "Cache looks like a hard place to make a living.''

Now Fannie scowled. "All the soldiers at the fort are broke and so are the cowboys who come through with the herds. Was afraid I'd have to stay here all winter. Unless some piece of good luck came my way." She looked directly at him as when she spoke.

"Good fortune comes when you least expect it. At least that's been my experience."

She brightened again. "And it comes in many different packages, I've learned. A smart person has to be able to recognize it when it comes along."

"That's true. It isn't always easy to identify."

"You have to look closer," she said just above a whisper. She placed a palm on his forearm. "Sometimes it's like a Christmas present. You have to take the outer wrapper off to be sure of what's inside."

Slocum recognized the suggestion she was making. He would enjoy taking off her outer wrapper—the green velvet dress—to see what was underneath. "I like unwrapping things," he said in a matter-of-fact way.

The barman brought them two more drinks and hurried off as soon as the money was securely in his hand.

Fannie's eyes settled on over the butt of his Colt. "Why do you carry a gun, Mr. Slocum? A man in the horse business doesn't need a gun, I shouldn't think."

"There are men who might try to take advantage of a traveler carrying money. I use the gun to discourage them. I usually have to carry cash to pay for the horses I acquire. I won't let any highwaymen take it from me."

She let the subject drop after hearing his explanation. "I want you to tell me everything about California. And most of all, about San Francisco."

"That's a tall order," he said. "California's a big place, and so is San Francisco. It could take all night to tell you all about it."

Fannie squeezed his arm. "I've got the time," she told him.

3

His second-story hotel room was at the back and had a window overlooking the roof of a harness shop. The narrow room was furnished with a washstand, a cracked mirror, and a bed with a lumpy cotton-ticking mattress. He surveyed his accommodations with passing interest. At least it was better than sleeping on the ground, he told himself.

He piled his gear in the corner, leaning his rifle against the water-stained wall paper. After seeing to the stabling of his stud, he was ready for a hot bath, a close shave, and several deep pulls on the bottle of pale whiskey he had bought at the Wagon Wheel, even though the contents reminded him of linament mixed with gunpowder.

Slocum was headed downstairs for the bathhouse behind the hotel when a commotion out in the street caught his attention. Two uniformed cavalrymen were talking to an angular cowboy with a badge pinned to his shirtfront. A crowd of curious citizens had gathered around them. One of the soldiers was speaking.

"Scalped 'em all, Sheriff, includin' the women. Worst mess I ever saw in my life. The captain in charge of one of our patrols coming from the south said they ran into a big bunch of runaway Comanches, so Major Thompson is sure it was Comanches who done this. The Major is orderin' three columns to divide up headed south. We'll find the murderin' redskins. Captain Carter said he'd recognize the bunch we run into. The Major wanted you to know we've got renegade Comanches on the loose, so you can warn folks to be on the lookout. Those Indians scalped five men an' two women. They'll be dangerous, so you might want to spread the word to settlers outside of town.''

''Damn,'' the Sheriff muttered, balling his hands into fists. ''I'll deputize a few men. We'll warn everybody to keep their guns handy. Just when it looks like most of the Indian troubles are over, somethin' like this happens. You say it was Comanches?''

''Captain Carter said they was. He ran into 'em comin' up from Childress, only they said they was just huntin' deer and buffalo.''

''Thanks for the warning, Sergeant. I'll get some men headed out to the ranches an' farms right away.''

Slocum couldn't believe his ears. The Kwahadies they met on the ride up to Fort Sill had not been looking for a fight, only something to feed their families. Slocum knew the Kwahadies and the other four Comanche tribes. When Comanches went on the warpath, they never took women along. The women he saw, including the beautiful Kwahadie chieftan's daughter, would not have accompanied a war party under any circumstances. What the sergeant just told the sheriff had to be wrong . . . unless another band of Comanches was the cause of the trouble.

Slocum turned back to the hotel. It couldn't be a Comanche massacre. Comanches never scalped women of any race. It was considered dishonorable for a man, a warrior, to take the hair of a female. The report the soldiers had given the sheriff had to be way off target. It was probably that tinhorn Captain Carter who was responsible, he thought. Carter didn't know one Indian from another. It had almost cost him and forty of his troopers their lives when Carter made ready to launch an attack on the Kwahadie hunting party.

• • •

With his clean clothes hanging on a wall peg, Slocum smoked a big cheroot and sipped at the bitter whiskey while seated in a cast-iron bathtub. He was enjoying himself. His thoughts strayed to the coming evening and the beautiful Fannie. He tried to imagine what she would look like naked. It had been too long without a woman in his bed, and an erection throbbed between his thighs. But pretty as Fannie was, she could not compare to the rare natural beauty of the Comanche girl. He wondered what she would be like making love beneath the stars. Try as he might, even with the anticipation of being with Fannie tonight, he couldn't shake the image of the Indian girl's from his mind.

But then his thoughts returned to the report he'd heard from the two troopers. Seven scalpings, including two women.

"No way Comanches did it," he muttered to himself. He had the bathhouse all to himself because it was early in the day. A black girl brought him buckets of hot water from time to time, and he idled away more than an hour sitting in soapy water that smelled sweetly of lilacs.

Eventually he climbed out of the tub and toweled himself off before putting on a fresh shirt, clean socks, and his best denim pants. Last of all, he tucked his .32 inside his shirt and buckled on his gunbelt.

At the hotel desk he inquired about a barbershop and was given directions westward down Main Street. Sauntering outside, Slocum felt better than he had in many days.

He strolled casually down the boardwalk toward the barber. Several men with saddle horses had gathered in front of the sheriff's office. They had holstered pistols and rifles in long-gun boots tied to their saddles. He counted almost a dozen men.

If it was a Comanche massacre, he thought, these cowboys and town folk didn't stand a chance against them.

• • •

The barber's name was Sam. He shaved Slocum's chin carefully while they talked.

"That's what everybody's sayin'," Sam said. "It was Comanches done it."

"It ain't likely," Slocum told him.

"How's that, mister?"

"I've had experience with Comanches over the years. They're brave people. They believe in honor and honorable warfare. They'd never scalp women under any circumstances. My money says it's somebody else who killed those settlers."

"But this Cap'n Carter said he saw 'em south of here, an' he swears it was Comanches."

"I was with Carter when he saw them, and they were Kwahadie Comanches. Trouble is, they had women with 'em. Comanches never take women along with a war party. I talked to the warrior who was leading them. I had to use sign language because that green captain didn't understand it and he didn't speak Comanche. The Indians told me how the army gives 'em spoiled meat, and it makes their children sick. They were hunting deer and buffalo when we ran into 'em, so their kids wouldn't go hungry."

"Did you tell that to Cap'n Carter?" Sam asked, scraping whisker stubble off Slocum's neck.

"I did. Sounds to me like he didn't believe it."

"You oughta tell what you know to the post commander before they go after the wrong bunch of Indians."

"It really isn't any of my affair, though I'd probably be saving the lives of a few local citizens and soldiers. I don't think either one wants to tangle with the Kwahadies if they're armed."

"But you said they was only huntin' . . ."

"They were. Otherwise there wouldn't have been any women with 'em."

"You should ride out to the fort an' tell Major Thompson what you just told me. Even if, like you say, it ain't

none of your affair. Might keep a lot of blood from bein'
spilled over a mistake.''

"I suppose I could," Slocum agreed. "I'll give it some
thought.''

Sam wiped the lather off his neck and cheeks. "We ain't
had no Indian troubles in quite a spell. Sure would be a
shame if we did for the wrong reason.''

Smelling of bay rum hair tonic, Slocum got out of the
chair and paid for his haircut and shave. "Keep the
change," he said on his way out the door, tugging his Stetson down in front.

"Sure wish you'd ride out to the fort an' tell that major
what you know," Sam added, pocketing his money. "Be
a damn shame if Cache had a bunch of funerals that wasn't
necessary.''

At a mercantile, he found a bottle of French wine and a
bundle of rum-soaked cigars. Walking the streets of Cache,
he tipped his hat to the ladies and took stock of the town.
Cache served as a waystation for travelers and a place
where the merchants who made their living off the Indian
reservation kept stores and shops. The small town had a
temporary look about it. Tents made up most of the business establishments, as if the proprietors were ready to
move on at a moment's notice.

Near the livery stable, he encountered a drummer in a
bowler hat and rumpled brown suit who was taking his
packs off the back of a mule.

"Howdy, mister," the drummer said to Slocum as he
was about to enter the barn to check on his stud. "Reckon
you heard 'bout them scalpins south of here.''

"I heard," Slocum replied.

"I saw it fer myself. Worst sight you ever saw. Blood
all over the ground.''

Slocum hesitated near the stable doors. "Someone said
two women were scalped.''

"It's a fact. One was mighty young. She coulda been

pretty, if it wasn't fer her hair bein' gone like it was. I seen her skullbone plain as day.''

"A soldier said the army thinks Comanches did it."

"Ain't no doubt, mister. They's the worst of the lot of 'em in my book, an' I've seen plenty."

"Comanches don't scalp women." Slocum spoke his words deliberately, with authority.

The drummer turned his ruddy face toward Slocum as he took down a pack from the mule's back. "Is that so? You don't have the look of a feller who knows Injuns."

"I've made the acquaintance of a few Comanches. Sometimes it was peaceable. Not always. They fight hard as hell, but they don't scalp women."

"The ones I seen at that creek was damn sure scalped plumb to the bone."

"Then it isn't likely Comanches did it."

The salesman dropped his pack on the ground near his feet with a curious look in his eye. "Who the hell else would have done somethin' terrible like that?"

"Maybe Osages or a Choctaw war party. They don't make that much of a distinction when it comes to ene- mies."

"You sound mighty damn sure."

"I am, on this particular topic. I did my share of scouting for the army a while back. I spent some time in Apache country, and before that I tracked some northern tribes. You can be pretty sure it wasn't Comanches who did what you say happened."

The drummer shook his head. "Either way, I'm stayin' in this lousy settlement till they find the bunch who done it. I ain't lookin' to lose my hair."

Slocum glanced into the stable. His Palouse was eating hay and its flanks were full. He was getting what he paid for when he gave the stablekeeper an extra dollar. A clean stall and oats, with plenty of fresh-cut prairie hay. "If it was me I wouldn't worry about it," he said, turning back in the direction of the Grand Hotel.

"And why's that, mister? I worry when I could be the next feller who goes bald afore his time."

"I doubt it'll happen again. If it was an Osage or Choctaw war party, they won't hang around to wait for the army to come after them."

"Just the same, I think I'll stay. You don't strike me as a feller who's all that sure of what he's sayin'."

"Suit yourself," Slocum said with a shrug, ambling off toward his room.

"By the way, mister . . . that's a gunfighter's rig you're wearin'. Are you, by chance, a shootist?"

Slocum did not bother to turn around. "I'm in the horse business. The gun is just for looks, in case some fool thinks he can take my poke."

"I'd be careful in this neck of the woods. It's full of men on the dodge from the law. Just a week ago I had three fellers ride up to my camp carryin' guns. If I hadn't stuck a twelve-gauge shotgun in their faces, they might have took everything I own."

"A man can't be too careful in Indian Territory," he said as he walked out of earshot.

"That's the damn truth," the drummer called out as he hoisted his packs.

Slocum put his mind back on the Indian girl. It would be a shame if a woman as beautiful as she was harmed by the cavalry in an attempt to punish whoever was responsible for the scalpings. One thing he was sure of: It wasn't Comanches who scalped the women.

His thoughts then returned to the business at hand: the seduction of a pretty redhead by the name of Fannie. He intended to wine her and dine her at the Palace tonight, and when the hour grew late, after she'd had several glasses of brandy, he meant to take her upstairs to his room at the Grand.

A red-orange sunset emblazoned the skies above Cache as he entered the hotel to climb to his room. A deep longing warmed his groin. If Miss Fannie gave her consent, she would be in for a long ride on his mattress tonight.

4

He waited for her over a glass of cognac, a watered-down version of one of his favorite drinks. But he was, he realized, lucky to find cognac of any description in Indian Territory.

She came through the door wearing a red dress. Her hair was done in curls, and a red ribbon was tied around her neck. She wore rouge and lip paint, and high-heeled shoes of the button variety.

He stood up as she walked to his table. "Good evening, Miss Fannie. You look lovely tonight." It seemed as if every head in the house turned when she entered the lamplit room.

"Why, thank you, Mr. Slocum. I do hope I haven't kept you waiting."

"I've been enjoying a glass of cognac. Will you have one with me?"

"Of course," she replied as he pulled back her chair.

The red gown revealed even more cleavage than her green velvet dress, and her creamy breasts jiggled as she settled herself and sat down. Her nipples were barely covered by the silky fabric.

He took his seat. "I'm glad you came. It would have been more proper for a gentleman to call for a lady at her residence, but I do understand about the rules at your board-inghouse.''

A waiter hurried over to take Fannie's order. ''What will the lady have, sir?''

''Cognac. And while you're here, get us two steaks, the best you have. The lady will tell you how she wants hers cooked and what she'll have with it.''

''Of course, sir.''

''I like mine rare,'' Fannie said, staring at him sugges-tively. ''Potatoes and any type of greens will be fine with me.''

''I like things rare myself,'' he said, after placing their order with their waiter. ''Rare women, women who are unusually beautiful, are my favorite, and they're quite rare, especially in an out-of-the-way place like Cache.''

''You have a way with words, Mr. Slocum.''

''Please call me John.''

''As you wish, John,'' she replied, slipping her shawl from her milky-white shoulders to drape it across the back of her chair.

''I've dreamed of being in San Francisco for so long,'' she said as she finished the last of her dessert. ''If I can only find a way to get there.''

''Perhaps I may be of some service. On occasion I do some work for the railroad.''

''What sort of work is that?'' she asked.

''They call it detective work. I make sure valuable ship-ments arrive at their destination. I might be able to convince someone at the Texas & Pacific to provide you with a com-plimentary ticket to California. I'd have to send a telegram to the main office to be sure. I'm not the sort to make empty promises.''

She reached for his hand. ''You are a true gentleman, John. Even if you can't arrange passage aboard a train for me, I won't hold it against you. You said you would try, and that's enough to convince me that you're a man with a good heart who cares about a woman in distress.''

"It's bad luck that you were left here in such difficult circumstances. It must be hard in a town like this on your own.''

She nodded and sipped more cognac. "I've done without a good many things.'' She turned and stared at him for a while before she spoke again. "More than anything else, I've done without a good man. I've been lonely.''

"Maybe I can also remedy that situation. If you won't think I'm being presumptious, we could take a walk down Main Street and go up to my room for a glass of wine. I purchased a bottle of the best they had, a French import.''

She smiled. "I think I'd like that. You won't think I'm being unladylike by accepting your offer?''

"Not at all,'' he told her, signaling the waiter for the bill. "I like a woman who knows what she wants. Being coy about it only makes things more difficult for both parties.''

"I agree,'' she said, pulling her shawl around her as she stood up. "One thing you can be certain of, John. I'm a woman who knows exactly what she wants.''

In the dim light cast by a small oil lamp on the washstand, Slocum poured Fannie a third glass of wine. A cool breeze wafted through the open window. They sat side by side on the bed talking about San Francisco. The room had no chairs, so the bed was the only place to sit.

"The Old Frisco Opera House is a sight to see,'' he told her. "It's the most elegant I've ever seen. You'll like it there. There are stage plays and operas and all manner of entertainment.''

"I'd do anything to get to San Francisco,'' she said, gazing deep into his eyes. "I wish you could be there with me when I see the city for the first time.''

"I'm afraid business will keep me elsewhere for the present. Perhaps next year, if things go well. But I'd be honored to be in your company most any place, Fannie. It wouldn't have to be San Francisco.''

She smiled. ''I can't help noticing how you look at me, at my bosom.''

''Does it make you uncomfortable?''

''Not at all,'' she murmured.

''I can honestly say I can't help myself. You have a magnificent chest . . . very large for a woman your size. It almost seems like your dress is too small to cover you. I find it very appealing.''

Fannie put down her glass. ''Would you care to see more?'' she asked. Reaching behind her as if she already knew the answer to her question, she began to work the buttons open.

''Of course,'' he replied. ''Let me help you with those back buttons.''

''You won't think I'm a loose woman if I take my dress off?''

''Quite the contrary. I'll think you're a woman who knows what she wants.''

Fannie stood up slowly and turned around so he could open her buttons down to her waist. She wriggled the dress over her hips and let it fall to the floor, until she was standing with her back to him wearing nothing but a corset and silk stockings. When she turned to face him, she was pulling the strings free on her corset in a slow, suggestive way. The twin mounds of her soft flesh bulged above the corset, until the lacing was loosened enough to allow her to tug it down off her breasts.

Her admired her bosom in silence for a moment. Its rosy-pink nipples were twisted hard and erect. ''How beautiful you are,'' he said as his cock began to swell.

''Do you want to see more?'' she asked playfully. A grin lifted the corners of her ruby lips, and her teeth sparkled in the lamplight.

''What a silly question.''

''I used to be very bashful. The first time I took my

clothes off in front of a man, my face got so hot I thought
I'd die.''

Slocum stood up to help her with the corset laces. "I'm
glad you got over it." He push the undergarment down over
her hips.

Fannie began rolling her stockings down. A mound of
flame-red hair glistened above her thighs.

"Sit down and I'll take off your shoes," he said, his
prick throbbing inside his pants.

She sat, and without an invitation she opened the top of
his denims, one brass fastener at a time. "Good grief," she
whispered, her voice thickening. "Are you really this . . .
big?"

She pulled his cock from the leg of his pants and gasped.
"It's almost too big. I've never seen one . . ."

"I'll use it real gentle," he promised, tossing one of her
shoes to the floor.

Fannie stroked his pulsing member. "I'm not sure I can
take all of it."

"We can try," he said, ridding her foot of the other shoe
and then pulling off both stockings.

"I suppose . . . we can," she stammered, and now her
breathing was quicker. She couldn't take her eyes from his
swollen cock, even as he unbuttoned his shirt, continuing
to stroke it gently with a slight tremor in her hand.

He sat on the edge of the mattress and pulled off his
boots and pants, tucking his bellygun into the top of one
stovepipe boot.

"Please turn down the lamp," Fannie whispered, swinging her legs off the floor so she lay flat on the bed, watching
him and his stiff cock with what could only be described
as fascination. "It's too bright in here."

He turned down the wick until it glowed pale and cast
faint shadows on the walls. Then he lay down beside her
and handed her a glass of wine. "Finish this, pretty lady,"
he said, cupping a hand over her left breast, gently pinching
the nipple between his thumb and forefinger.

Fannie downed her drink in a single swallow.

He emptied his own glass and placed them both on the washstand before returning his hand to her breast.

"Oh, that feels good," she sighed, momentarily closing her eyes. She reached for his prick and found it, clasping it in a firm grip while he kneaded her breast.

He bent over her face and kissed her gently. "You are a very passionate women, I can tell." He released her nipple and moved his hand down to her cunt, noticing at once how wet it was when his finger slid across her soft mound.

"That feels even better," she moaned, tightening the muscles in her thighs while spreading her legs apart.

Slocum entered her with his finger and she gasped with delight.

"I want more," Fannie panted, her breath coming in short, quick bursts.

He rolled between her curved thighs and placed the head of his cock against the lips of her cunt, hesitating, applying no pressure.

"I hope it's not too big," she groaned, beginning slow, rhythmic thrusts against him. "Clyde was small, if you know what I mean. I don't know if I can take you inside me."

"You told me before you liked men rough, but in a gentle sort of way. Just relax. I'll show you how."

He pushed into her mound only slightly, parting the wet lips a fraction.

"I do like it rough," she gasped, "but you must promise me you won't hurt me."

"You have my word, Fannie."

Her pelvic thrusts became harder, faster, as though she meant to drive herself onto his prick in spite of the resistance he felt. "I want more," she hissed, clenching her teeth.

With subtle pressure he pushed another inch of his thick cock inside her.

"That feels wonderful!" she exclaimed, raising her voice

as her hunching grew faster, stronger, more urgent. "Push harder, John! Harder!"

Again he sent more of his prick into her, feeling her wetness and heat. Her body was trembling from head to toe and she dug her fingernails into his back.

Slocum's balls began to rise, his jism ready to explode if he allowed it. He intended to satisfy her first, before he had his own release.

"More!" Fannie cried, drawing blood where her fingernails cut his skin. Thrusting, hunching, she placed her heels behind his knees and locked him in a powerful leg embrace.

He felt the walls of her cunt open slightly, and when they did he drove his prick into her with a bit more force than he'd intended.

"Oh! Oh!" Fannie gasped, slamming the lips of her mound against the thickness of his shaft. "I'm going to come, John! I'm going to come!"

Her entire body shook so violently he gripped the headboard with both hands to keep from being thrown to the floor while she rocked back and forth underneath him, groaning, panting, her skin moist with perspiration.

Bedsprings creaked with the power of their lovemaking, and the iron headboard banged against the wall when Fannie finally reached her climax. She stiffened, arching her back off the mattress, screwing her eyelids tightly shut.

Slocum waited for her to relax. "That's a good girl," he said gently, returning to his own slow thrusting. "Now we go for the second act of this play. Close your eyes and pretend you're at the Old Frisco Opera House now."

She returned his thrusts with pelvic movements of her own, a grinding motion, and the wet sounds of his prick sliding in and out of her cunt were hard to hear above her gasps for more air.

His tempo increased and the tip of his prick felt warm, ready to erupt.

When he reached his climax, the sensation spread from his balls to his thighs, then all over his body. After a few more thrusts he lay still, breathing hard, smiling.

5

Fort Sill lay on a flat plain northwest of Cache. It consisted of a collection of wooden barracks, a parade ground and headquarters building, a sutler's store, and rows of stables surrounded by corrals holding hundreds of horses. Beyond the army post, buffalo-hide lodges and crude cabins stretched as far as the eye could see. Smoke rose from cooking fires into a cloudless sky. The Indians were preparing smoked meat—the only way to preserve it for the coming winter.

It had been difficult for Slocum to decide whether or not to ride out to the fort to tell the commanding officer what he knew about the Kwahadie hunting party they'd encountered on the way up from Texas. It truly wasn't any of his affair, and yet he felt some responsibility. Captain Carter knew so little about Indians, Kwahadies in particular, that he'd given the fort commander an inaccurate picture of the danger he believed existed at the hands of what Slocum felt sure was only a party of hunters.

He rode toward post headquarters at a walk, keeping the stud in check on a tight rein. A squad of infantrymen marched across the parade ground carrying rifles. At the stables, he could see cavalrymen saddling horses. No doubt a patrol was being mounted to look for the Kwahadies.

"Typical of the army," Slocum muttered, wondering how the cavalry ever caught up to any Indians when they waited to begin a search until the sun was already an hour above the horizon.

He was wearing a beaded buckskin shirt, and it drew a few stares as he rode across the parade ground to dismount in front of the headquarters building. Slocum had chosen the shirt in part because there was a chill in the air, a warning of the cold weather to come in the days ahead. The deerskin shirt had been given to him by a Ute warrior he found mortally wounded in the lower Rockies a few years earlier. He had made the Indian as comfortable as possible until the bullet hole in his gut finally claimed his life. Slocum treasured the garment, which reminded him of the special bond that had developed between him and the dying warrior.

He tied off the stud at a hitchrail and climbed the steps to the front door. Two soldiers wearing privates' stripes blocked his way.

"I'd like to talk to Major Thompson," he began. "I've got some information about those Indians he's looking for."

"Step inside and speak to Sergeant Brooks at the desk. He will ask the major if he can see you now."

Slocum nodded and went inside. A long front room ran the length of the building. At the desk guarding the door of the back office, a burly sergeant regarded his Indian shirt with disdain.

"What do you want?" the sergeant asked, as he took in Slocum's cross-pull gunbelt.

"I'd like a word with Major Thompson. I saw those Indians he's after. Got a few things I want to tell him that might be a help."

"What's your name, mister?"

"Slocum. John Slocum."

"Wait here, Mr. Slocum. I'll tell the major you're here."

Sergeant Brooks was only in the major's office a few

moments before he returned. "Go on in, Mr. Slocum. Major Thompson said he had a few minutes."

Slocum walked into a sparsely furnished office. A man in his late fifties with a handlebar mustache and sideburns sat behind a desk. He gave Slocum a wary look.

"What's this I hear about you knowing where we can find the Comanche renegades?" Thompson asked, without extending his hand or offering Slocum a seat.

Slocum took an immediate dislike to the man. "The ones we saw just north of the Red weren't renegades, Major. They were a hunting party. They had five women with them. Kwahadies never take women along when they're making war. I spoke with their leader. He said they were hunting deer or buffalo. That their children were hungry because the beef they got here had worms in it. Those Comanches were peaceful, or we'd have never made it out of there alive. That young captain—his name was Carter—couldn't read sign talk. I explained to him that those Indians weren't looking for a fight. They were simply real hungry. That's why they left the reservation."

Thompson cocked his head. There was doubt on his face. "Where do you get all this special knowledge about Comanches? It sounds like bullshit to me. Comanches are the worst of all our charges here at Fort Sill. They cause more trouble than all the rest of 'em put together."

Slocum shrugged and turned away from the major's desk. He was ready to leave after these insulting remarks. "I scouted for Crook and a few others some years ago, but if you think all I'm giving you is bullshit, this conversation is over."

"Hold on just a minute, Mr. Slocum," Thompson said. His voice had changed. "I didn't know you were an experienced scout. Sorry for what I said. Have a chair. I'll tell Sergeant Brooks to bring us some coffee."

With some reluctance, Slocum returned to the desk and accepted the hand Major Thompson offered him.

"I served under General Crook," the major said by way

of apology. "I didn't sleep much last night after learning about those scalpings. Tell me about those Comanches you ran across and why you think they were peaceful. I'll listen, and if you've got any ideas about who killed the settlers, I'd like to hear that too."

Slocum settled into a hardbacked wooden chair while Thompson leaned through the doorway to send the sergeant for coffee. It was possible, Slocum decided, that Thompson would listen to reason.

The major returned to his desk and began packing a briarwood pipe with tobacco.

"First off, like I said before, Comanches don't take women on raiding parties," Slocum began.

"I never heard that before," Thompson said. "You mentioned they had five women?"

"I was told one was the daughter of a Kwahadie chief. She was a pretty thing."

Hearing this, Major Thompson smiled, puffing on his pipestem to get the tobacco going. "That'll be Senatey. She's the daughter of Chief Lame Bear. Every soldier at this fort wants to fuck her as soon as they lay eyes on her." He chuckled. "She's without a doubt the prettiest Indian woman I ever saw, but she won't have anything to do with a white man, and it's against standing orders for any of my soldiers to . . . consort with an Indian, if you know what I mean. Hell, I'd like to hump her myself, only it's damn sure against regulations. A man could get court-martialed for even *trying* to fuck her. Besides that, her father is one of the bloodiest Indian criminals we have on this post. He's in the guardhouse now, chained up. We have to keep him there or he'll run off. They say Lame Bear killed more than a hundred whites himself, before Quannah agreed to the treaty. Lame Bear is gonna stay behind bars, as far as I'm concerned, unless the big brass orders me to let him go for some reason."

"Senatey is her name?" Slocum asked. He wanted to be sure of it.

"I don't know what it means in English, but that's her Comanche name."

"It means 'warrior woman,' " Slocum told him. "It's a name given only to the daughter of a great warrior. Back in the old days, when the Kwahadies were down in Palo Duro Canyon, there was another woman named Senatey. I remember her. I was with McKenzie's troops when they captured Buffalo Hump and the last of the wild Kwahadies. It was one hell of a fight even though those Indians were outnumbered ten to one. They earned a lot of respect from Ranald McKenzie and General George Crook that day. General Crook refused to kill the survivors when they ran out of bullets. He told McKenzie that any man, regardless of his color, who'd fight that hard when they knew they were licked, deserved to live."

"You are obviously well-versed in Kwahadie practices, Mr. Slocum. If you believe the Kwahadies you saw were merely out hunting game, then what happened to those settlers? We had a roll call yesterday. Took all day to get it done. None of the other Indians are missing. The Indian who led the bunch you and Captain Carter met is a warrior by the name of Conas. Again, I don't know what it means in English. Nor does it matter, I suppose."

"It's the Comanche word for fire."

"Then you also speak a great deal of their language, it would seem."

"Some. It's been a spell since I used it. The main thing to remember is that a Comanche won't scalp a woman. I've known members of all five tribes . . . the Kotsotekas, the Noconas, the Yamparikas. None of 'em scalp women. It's a form of dishonorable conduct, showing cowardice. Whoever scalped the women, it wasn't Comanches."

Thompson frowned. "Then who the hell do we look for?" he asked, puffing furiously on his pipe.

"If it was me, I'd look for tracks around the spot where those folks were killed. Follow 'em to see what direction they went afterward."

"I don't have a decent tracker among my Pawnee scouts. It seems they've found a way to get their hands on whiskey. Most of them are drunks. Utterly useless. I've requested permission to send them home."

"Surely you can find someone who can read horse sign?"

"I've tried. Finding a sober man is the hardest part. An Indian seems to have a natural gift for that sort of thing, but the free Indians around here are all drunks or loafers who won't take an offer of pay from the army to help us catch the other Indians when they escape from the reservation."

They heard Sergeant Brooks clumping across the floor of the outer office with the coffee.

"I don't suppose you'd be interested in a short-term job as my scout?" the major asked.

"I've got pressing business elsewhere, Major. Sorry."

"I wish you'd reconsider."

He remembered the Comanche girl, her rare beauty and the way she looked at him with the hint of a smile on her face. "I wish I could help. Let me think on it a spell. I'll let you know tonight or tomorrow morning. The most I'd be willing to do is get your troopers headed in the right direction."

"The pay isn't much, but I'd be grateful for any help a man with your experience would be willing to give us. Anything is better than what I've got. A bunch of drunk Pawnees who don't earn what little money we're paying them."

"I'm real familiar with army scouting pay, Major. It's just enough to keep a man from starving."

Thompson nodded. "At least you'd be helping us bring the killers to justice. I'll see to it that they're prosecuted to the full extent of the law. Keep in mind that two women were murdered in the most brutal way possible."

"I said I'd think on it. I was headed back up to Denver on business."

"I do hope you'll give it serious consideration before you refuse."

After a polite knock on the door, Slocum was offered a tin cup of coffee by Sergeant Brooks. It tasted bitter, the result of scorched coffee beans. As Brooks left the office, he closed the door behind him.

"Tell me more about Senatey. Conas told me in sign she was the property of another man."

Thompson slurped his coffee noisily before replying. "It's an odd Comanche habit, one I don't fully understand. Perhaps you will. When we put Chief Lame Bear in the guardhouse, the girl was given to her uncle for what amounts to safekeeping. If my memory serves me correctly, her uncle's name is Quahip. He is responsible for her until she takes a husband. These Comanches seem to trade women, even their own daughters, as if they were pieces of property."

Slocum was pleased to learn that the girl was not yet married, but he couldn't say why. Senatey showed no interest in white men, the major had said. "They do have some strange customs."

Now the major grinned. "You're as attracted to her as the men at this fort, aren't you?"

"She's a beautiful woman."

"Our Indian agent, Mr. Tatum, informs me that she hates all white men for what they have done to her people, for forcing them to live on a reservation. She speaks some English, they say, but she refused to attend the school we set up to teach them our ways. Of all the tribes gathered here, Comanches have been the most difficult to civilize."

"I doubt that anyone will ever civilize them to our ways. They value their freedom more than most."

"So it would seem. But I hope you'll agree to do some tracking for us. If you're right about the Comanche practice—that they never scalp women—it would be a shame to punish them for something they didn't do. My superiors will demand it unless the real culprits are caught."

"I'll let you know," Slocum said, leaving the rest of his scorched coffee untouched. "Thanks for your time, Major. I'll be in touch with you by tomorrow morning, one way or the other."

6

Fannie was still asleep with the curtains pulled across the window of Slocum's room when he got back to the hotel at nine-thirty. She stirred when she heard him come in.

"Is that you, John?" she asked sleepily. The bedsheet barely covered her twin mountains of white flesh. Her long red hair was spread over the pillow, and the outline of her body beneath the sheet clung to her every curve. She stretched lazily and yawned as he closed the door.

"It's me. I rode out to the fort to have a word with Major Thompson about that Indian attack. I may stay in Cache a couple of days to help the army find whoever's responsible. At least long enough to put 'em on their tracks."

Fannie smiled and raised her head off the pillow. "That means you'll be here a while longer. I'm glad. You made me feel so good last night. I'm a little sore in a special place, but it was worth it. You have the biggest cock, and what's more important, you know how to use it."

He hung his hat on a wall peg, recalling last night's romp with Fannie. "Allow me to return the compliment. You're a hell of a good lover. You make just the right moves." Slocum took off his gunbelt and looped it around a bedpost at the foot of the bed. "I like a woman who truly enjoys what she's doing."

Fannie tossed the sheet aside and swung her feet off the bed. Her eyes were fastened on Slocum's crotch. "Come over here just a minute," she said huskily. "I'll show you something else I truly enjoy."

He'd promised the major he'd be ready to lead a squad of the more experienced cavalrymen down to the scene of the massacre in less than an hour, but right then he couldn't think of a better way to spend that time. "I thought you said you were sore in one spot, that 'special' place."

"I am," she whispered, reaching for the top button of his pants. "It isn't the only place I enjoy the feel of a stiff prick. I'll show you. Clyde said I had a talent for what I'm about to do to you."

He felt his cock thicken as her fingers reached into his pants. Slocum stood at the edge of the bed where she was sitting while she slowly drew out his hardening member. "I think I'm gonna like this," he said, certain of what she was about to do.

Fannie took the tip of his cock into her mouth, lightly flicking her tongue back and forth across his glans. His prick responded at once, filling with blood as pleasure awakened in his groin.

She took more of him into his mouth, beginning to bob her head up and down.

"That feels mighty good," he told her, listening to the soft sucking sounds that came from between her lips.

Gradually, she increased the speed of her talented tongue, almost wrapping it around his shaft.

"The gambler was right," he said, his balls rising. "You do have a talent for this."

Now her sucking sounds became louder, the pressure from her tongue harder, more demanding. He glanced down at her breasts and saw hardened nipples. What she was doing excited her. The proof of it was jutting from each rounded breast.

Slocum began thrusting deeper into her mouth, gently so as not to choke her, feeling his jism begin its ascent. The muscles in his buttocks tightened in anticipation, and Fannie recognized it at once. She took a cheek of his ass in each hand and pulled him closer, grabbing his flesh with her fingers.

Seconds later his jism spurted into her mouth. Waves of pleasure raced through him and he groaned softly, continuing to come in shorter bursts until his balls emptied.

Fannie gulped and swallowed, sucking harder than ever as the last of his seed was spent.

He stood there a moment, weakkneed, as the feeling of utter ecstasy slowly faded. Fannie continued to suck his cock, yet it was gentler now, until at last she pulled back, looking up at him, smiling.

"Was it okay?" she asked, searching his face.

"It was better than just okay, pretty lady. You have a real talented tongue. Clyde must have been out of his head to up and leave you like he did. A woman who can suck a cock as well as you do is real damn hard to find."

"Are you going to leave me too?" she asked, as her smile faded. She held his limp cock in her hand, milking the last of his jism onto the floor.

Slocum knew he couldn't tell her the entire truth now. "I am gonna help you, Fannie. You said you wanted to see San Franciso more than anything in the world. I'm gonna see to it that you get there. When my business in Denver is wrapped up, I'll do my best to get out there to see you real soon. And I won't be leaving Cache for a few days, looks like. I promised I'd help Major Thompson look for whoever scalped those folks south of here. After I've done all I can for the army, I'll take you as far as the closest railroad. And I'll book passage for you to Santa Fe, maybe even all the way to California. It kinda depends."

"Depends on what?" she asked.

He grinned down at her. "On how many more talents you've got and how well you use them."

"I'll do anything, John. Just tell me, or show me what you want. I swear I'll do it." She averted her eyes briefly.

"I'm not a bad woman, you know. I'm doing this because I'm very attracted to you. You're a handsome man and the best lover a woman could want. I don't want you to think I'm cheap or a trashy kind of woman simply because I made love to you. I did it because I wanted to."

"No other possibility even crossed my mind," he told her in a gentle voice. But at the same time, he was wondering. Fannie was experienced. Maybe she was only using him to get to San Francisco. He decided it didn't matter. He could send a wire to Tom Ford at the Texas & Pacific and most likely get Fannie a ticket to wherever she wanted to go. Slocum had helped Ford safeguard some valuable shipments of gold, when an army payroll was consigned to the railroad a few years back. Five dead outlaws plus two more in a prison cell had been enough to convince Ford he'd picked the right man to guard the gold.

"I'll make love to you whenever you want, John," Fannie promised. "And if you really like what I just did to you, I'll do that too." She smiled again. "To tell the truth I enjoy doing it. It makes me hot, although I'm not sure why. A couple of times I've actually come myself while I've got a cock in my mouth. I know that sounds strange, but when a man comes it makes me come sometimes."

"You didn't come this time," he observed.

"I almost did. I was still half asleep when you got back. If you'll give me another chance . . ." She lifted his limp prick and put it between her lips again, jacking blood into his member with her hand while her tongue went back to work.

Slocum forgot about the time, the hour he said he needed before he rode back to the fort. The Major and the army would have to wait. Slowly, another erection hardened in Fannie's mouth.

With her other hand, she parted the tuft of red hair over her mound and started rubbing gently up and down between the lips of her cunt. A throaty groan came from deep inside her chest as she pleased herself, all the while stimulating him with her wet tongue, and the movement of her moist lips, sucking harder and faster as her pleasure heightened.

Just minutes later, he again filled her mouth with his seed. He was totally spent, weakened but content. At almost the same instant, Fannie gripped the base of his prick and stiffened with a climax of her own, trembling and moaning around a mouthful of cock and jism.

"You sure as hell know how to please a man," he said, after she milked him dry and licked the top of his cock clean.

"Only a special man," she replied. "If your cock wasn't so big I'd take it all in my mouth. There simply isn't room . . ."

Twelve cavalrymen rode in a paired column behind him. They were older men, veterans of earlier Indian campaigns, Major Thompson had assured him as they left the fort. The troop commander was a grizzled sergeant named Lee Watson, a forty-year-old cavalryman who was at Fort Grant in Arizona Territory during some of the worst Apache difficulties. Watson rode a horse like a man seasoned to a saddle and life out in the open.

"I figured same as you, Mr. Slocum," he said as they rode south toward the Red River. "Damn few Injuns will scalp a woman under any circumstance. Specially not a Comanch', cause they figure it shows a man's yellow to lift a woman's hair."

"That's been my experience with 'em too," Slocum said. "I feel real sure some other bunch is behind this. We'll know when we find their tracks. If we don't find any tracks at all, then it's possible they were Comanches."

"No tracks at-all?"

"A Comanche is the best horseman on earth, Sergeant. They know how to hide their tracks better'n anybody. I've seen 'em sweep the ground with mesquite branches for two or three miles behind their horses, just to wipe away any trace of a horse's prints. When they're wanting to stay hidden, they ride across every stretch of rock they come to so there won't be any horse sign to follow. A man's gotta get down on his hands and knees to see where a barefoot Comanche pony has crossed a slab of limestone.''

"I know they's tricky bastards all right, an' real hard to kill in a fight.''

"That's what I tried to explain to young Captain Carter on the ride up here. When we rode up on that bunch of fifty or sixty Kwahadies, the damn fool reached for his pistol. If I hadn't stopped him, he could have gotten all of us killed.''

"I just met Carter yesterday. He's a kid from Ohio. He wouldn't know which end of a polecat gives off stink. That's the trouble with this army these days. They sign all these kids to short hitches now. By the time they learn how to stay alive in Injun country, their hitch is over an' here comes another batch of raw recruits. It's a goddamn wonder ain't all of 'em dead as fence posts.''

"I reckon it's because the army doesn't need experienced soldiers any longer," Slocum said. "No more wars to fight. Most of the Indian tribes are on reservations now. Nothing much for a horseback soldier to do except keep an eye on 'em.''

"You got it figured right, Mr. Slocum. We ain't really soldiers no more.''

Slocum didn't mention how glad he was not to be a soldier anymore. Fighting for a losing cause as a Confederate all those years had taken all the soldiering out of him. He'd lost a brother to that war, and a part of his soul too, he reckoned. The last thing John Slocum would ever do again is put on any kind of uniform.

He shifted the subject. "Who found the settlers first?''

"Seems I heard it was a couple of cowboys comin' back from a trail drive to Kansas. One of 'em rode back toward the fort an' run into one of our patrols. He told where to find 'em an' then he headed back down to the river. Sergeant Steven and Corporal Baker was the first soldiers there. A burial detail went back down to dig the holes.''

Slocum frowned. An army burial detail would leave shod hoofprints all over the place, possibly hiding the trail the killers left behind. It meant he would have to ride bigger circles to find the escape route of the culprits, if he could find any trace of them at all.

He'd promised Major Thompson to do the best he could to lead a patrol in the right direction. But with the trail grown cold by now, the cavalry would be days behind the killers.

"It ain't far now," Sergeant Watson said, pointing to a row of low hills dotted with red oak and maple. The leaves were turning bright red, yellow, and brown as fall deepened. A brisk wind came at their backs, and Slocum thought he detected some moisture in it.

The search for the killers would come to an abrupt end if the rain came. It would wash out whatever tracks were still left to follow. But when he looked over his shoulder to the north and west, he saw clear skies behind them.

To pass the time, he thought about what Fannie had done when he returned to his room this morning. She was one hell of a woman. Not the least bit bashful. When he got back, he had to send a wire to the railroad asking for Mr. Ford's personal attention to a pressing matter. He wouldn't need to explain why he needed the ticket for Fannie. Tom Ford had been a good friend over the years and he wouldn't ask.

But then, oddly enough, with his thoughts still on Fannie, Slocum found himself remembering the Comanche girl, Senatey. It was rare to find an Indian woman, or a woman of any breed, who took his fancy so abruptly. It wasn't the eye-catching way she was dressed. Hell, she wore a dirty piece of fringed deerskin and not much else. It was her face, something about her dark brown eyes when she looked at him, that made his heart beat a little faster.

He wondered if he would ever see her again. It was not likely. And Major Thompson said she hated white men for what they had done to her people. He decided that it was best to put Senatey out of his mind for good.

7

Two log cabins sat beside a creek in a shallow valley beyond the hills. As Slocum rode out of the trees on a crest above the cabins, small barns, and pole corrals, Sergeant Watson signaled a halt.

"You can see them graves on the slope behind that shed, the fresh mounds of dirt an' all."

"I see 'em," Slocum replied, counting seven wooden crosses at the head of the graves. "If this was an Indian massacre, they would have burned those cabins down, most likely. Let's take a closer look, and tell your men to stay in formation so we don't add to the tracks left by that burial detail. I'll ride circles until I pick up any sign of unshod ponies." He frowned. "What don't make sense is why they slaughtered those people and left everything else alone. I reckon they stole their livestock, if they had any worth stealing. All those pole corrals are empty. Two wagons behind the sheds. You can see by the looks of things these folks didn't have much. Makes it hard to understand why a party of Indians would bother. If it was Indians to start with."

"Who the hell else would scalp 'em?" Watson asked.

"I haven't got an answer. Don't reckon we'll know till we find whoever did it."

He heeled his Palouse off the rise at a walk, puzzled by what they found. Two homesteads were left untouched, yet seven people, including two women, were scalped. When the Indians that Slocum had experience with wanted white settlers off their traditional hunting ground, they burned everything to the ground to discourage more whites from taking up residence. This was beginning to look like something other than an Indian massacre. But, like Sergeant Watson, Slocum couldn't fathom who would want to have Indians blamed for what happened here.

The first cabin was a two-room affair with a dog run. Nothing but logs chinked with mud and a sod roof to protect its owners from the weather. The door to the cabin stood open. On part of the rough-hewn split-log porch, dried bloodstains showed where a settler had lost his life.

Slocum gave the ground around the cabin a cursory inspection. Then he returned to Watson. "Have your men dismount and see if they can find anything inside, like personal effects, that'll tell us who these folks were. No names on any of the grave markers."

Sergeant Watson gave the order to dismount. Slocum eased his stud away from the cabin to begin riding widening circles around the valley until he found hoofprints.

He rode past the graves, then eastward toward land that was open and easier to travel. This was the most likely direction for attackers to leave in a hurry. Despite the beautiful fall colors in the trees around him, he felt gloomy. He imagined that he could hear the last sounds heard on this spot: the screams and cries of dying men and women.

It would require patience and an experienced eye to find any tracks. In this type of country, the grass grew thick. Only the rare barren spots would reveal any clues, and even then they would appear only if the killers were careless men.

At a tiny stream half a mile east of the cabins, he swung down to examine some prints in the soft mud at the edge of the streambed. Some of the tracks were two-toed animals, no doubt cattle stolen by the murderers after the raid.

And then he found what he was looking for—the prints of a dozen or more unshod horses.

''Big, for pony tracks,'' he muttered to himself.

The prints were headed due east. Here was a trail to follow, as he'd known all along there would be. Men of every other race left proof of their passing in open land. Only the Comanche seemed to understand that their tracks were as clear as a signpost pointing in their direction.

He mounted his stud and swung back to inform Sergeant Watson of his findings. As he'd agreed, Slocum would guide the patrol along the trail of the killers for a while, but not for long. He would put a cavalry unit on the right track behind whoever had slaughtered the settlers. The rest would be up to the army. Thompson had sent patrols in three directions, spread out in a triad to cover as much territory as possible. With the information Slocum provided to Sergeant Watson, they could follow the tracks all the way back to the killers' lair.

He held his stud in an easy lope, galloping back toward Fort Sill while Watson's cavalrymen followed the hoofprints. Slocum's job was done. He had done all he'd promised to do. But as he rode between a pair of heavily wooded knobs, he heard voices coming from a deep thicket off to the west. Men's voices and then a woman's scream.

He swung the Palouse in the direction of the cries and asked it for a hard gallop, opening his coat for an easier reach in case he needed his pistol in a hurry. The woman's shriek was plainly one of pain or fear. He wondered if the same killers who had attacked the cabins were about to claim more victims.

When he entered the forest, he was shocked by what he saw. In a small clearing about a quarter mile ahead, he saw three uniformed troopers surrounding a naked copper-skinned woman who was bound by ropes to a tree trunk.

The soldiers were laughing, taunting the girl, and playing with her breasts and her cunt.

One of the soldiers heard his horse. He wheeled around just as Slocum rode into view at the edge of the clearing. When the trooper saw that he was a white man, he lowered the pistol he was holding in his fist and grinned.

Slocum reined his Palouse to a halt. He looked at the woman for just an instant before he glared down at the trooper. "What the hell are you doing to her?" he demanded. Suddenly he was sure he recognized her. He looked at her again. A trickle of blood ran from her nose, and more blood surged from the edges of her mouth. He recognized Senatey.

"We caught her takin' a bath naked in that creek yonder," the soldier replied. "She ain't supposed to be off the reservation. So we tied her up."

Slocum turned back in the soldier's direction with a hard stare. "I saw what you were doing to her. It's enough to get you a damn court-martial, soldierboy. Now cut her loose. I'm headed back to Fort Sill to report directly to Major Thompson. I want your name and the names of these other yellow bastards."

"How do you know the major?" the soldier asked defiantly.

"He hired me to find whoever was responsible for scalping those settlers south of here, if it's any of your goddamn business. Cut her ropes and do it now! Otherwise I may be forced to take more drastic measures."

"You can't give me no orders, mister. You're a civilian. I only take orders from officers. An' I don't believe nothin' you said 'bout bein' hired by Major Thompson."

Slocum swung down before the trooper was finished with his protest. "I'll show you where I get my authority," he said in an even, controlled voice.

He stepped forward within arm's reach of the soldier's jaw, and before the corporal knew what was happening,

Slocum's fist went slamming into his left cheek, cracking bone when his knuckles landed.

He staggered back and slumped to the grass on his butt just as Slocum drew his .44, aiming it at the other two cavalrymen. "Untie the goddamn ropes!" he shouted, cocking his pistol. "I'll shoot the first son of a bitch who don't do exactly as I say!"

"Yessir," the youngest man stammered. He ran behind the tree to untie Senatey.

Now Slocum aimed his gun down at the sore-jawed corporal. "Get on your feet, soldierboy. Go fetch me a horse for this girl to ride and don't be slow about it. If you aren't back in five minutes with a horse, I'm gonna start shooting your friends here, one at a time. I'll tell Major Thompson they were about to rape this woman, and I had no choice but to kill 'em. Then I'll come looking for you, Corporal, with or without your name. And you can be damn sure I'll put a bullet through you same as I will the two boys over yonder. Now give me your name, or I'll just start shooting now and explain to the major later."

"I'm Dave Sims," the soldier said softly, rubbing his chin. "Them two's Jacobs an' Woods."

"Go fetch the horse," Slocum demanded. "One of you is gonna walk back to Fort Sill, and I don't give a damn which one it is."

"Yessir," the corporal mumbled, staggering off toward the trees south of the clearing.

Slocum started over to Senatey. Her torn deerskin dress was lying near her feet. He picked it up and handed it to her as the soldiers untied the ropes. She covered herself quickly, lowering her eyes, then wiped the blood off her lips and chin with her forearm. A large purple bruise swelled on her cheek and there were other dark red marks on her face.

He spoke to the two remaining soldiers. "You so make damn sure Sims gets me that horse for this woman. Don't test me to see if I mean what I say about putting bullet holes in you."

"Yessir," the young private said, taking off in a trot followed by the other trooper. "Don't you worry, sir. We'll be back with that horse right quick."

He let them go and turned back to the naked girl. "I'm sorry for what they did to you," he said. "Do you understand? I only speak a few words of *Sata Teichas.*" *Sata Teichas* was the Comanche tongue.

"I . . . know what you say," she said to him, trying to cover her breasts and groin with her dress.

"Hie hites," he told her, meaning that it was good and he was a friend.

She made no move to put on her dress. "How you know *Sata Teichas, Tosi Tivo?*"

She had addressed him with the Comanche word for a white man. "I learned some a long time ago. I forgot most of it by now."

"Why you help me?" she asked, looking into his eyes with a strange expression on her face.

Slocum glanced over his shoulder in the direction the three soldiers had gone. "Because you needed my help. All *Tosi Tivo* are not like those soldiers. Some of us are friends to the *Sata Teichas.* You are a woman. It doesn't matter what color you are. Men who aren't cowards don't abuse a woman under any circumstances."

"I see you before," she said, "with other soldiers."

"I remember. Major Thompson told me your name was Senatey, a warrior woman."

She gave him a weak smile.

"How did you get separated from the others, the hunters led by Conas?"

"Conas say we must go back. Too many soldiers. Bad thing happen."

"What kind of bad thing?"

She seemed hesitant to tell him.

"What was it?" he asked.

"Many bad men kill *Tosi Tivo*. We see bad men. Conas say army will say we do bad thing. He send me and other women back to Stinking Place."

"Stinking Place?"

"In *Tosi Tivo* say 'reservation.' "

Slocum grinned. The reservation did have a bad smell to it, the smell of too many people crowded together in too small a space. "Who were these bad men?"

Senatey frowned. "I can no say word in *Tosi Tivo*. They be men who take hair, take scalp for money."

"Mexican scalp hunters?" he asked.

She gave him a blank look. "Senatey no say word. Bad men who take hair."

He wondered if Mexican scalp hunters could have come this far north to look for trophy scalps. In Mexico, in Monterrey, he had heard Indian scalps were bringing as much as five dollars apiece. But the settlers who were scalped at the cabins were white. Her explanation didn't give him much to go on, not enough to convince Major Thompson this wasn't the work of the Comanches.

"Put on your dress," he told her. "I'll take you back to the fort, the Stinking Place, so you'll be safe."

She turned her back on him to step into her garment.

"What happened to the other *Sata Teichas* women who were with you?" he asked.

"All run away. *Tosi Tivo* soldiers shoot our ponies. We run and hide. Soldiers find me."

"I'll report what they did to Major Thompson. No one will harm you now. I'll make sure you get back safely."

"Why you do this for Senatey?" It was as though she couldn't believe a white man would do anything to help her.

"Because you need help and because the *Sata Teichas* are my friends."

With her dress covering her magnificent body, Senatey turned to face him. "You different. No be bad man."

"All white men aren't bad, Senatey. Some of 'em will

take advantage of a woman. You had the bad luck to meet up with three soldiers who need a lesson in manners.''

"I no understand. What is manner . . . s?"

He grinned again. "I'll explain on the way back to the fort . . . to the Stinking Place.''

When she looked at him now, he sensed she was beginning to trust him.

8

Off to the west he heard the sounds of running horses. He knew what it meant.

"Those soldiers took off," Slocum growled, looking in the direction of the hoofbeats. "Damn! I shouldn't have trusted 'em to bring a horse back. When I get to the fort, it'll be my word against theirs as to what happened here. They played me for a damn fool. . . ."

"I walk," Senatey said. "They kill all ponies where we take bath in stream."

"I oughta go after 'em," he said, realizing now he'd been hoodwinked by the three cavalrymen, who wanted to avoid a court-martial if Slocum brought charges.

He let out a sigh and turned back to the girl. "Where are the other *Sata Teichas* women who were with you?" he asked.

Senatey appeared to have trouble with his question. "Other women?"

"The four Conas sent back to the reservation after the bad men showed up. They were with you before."

"Run. I no see after *Tosi Tivo* chase me away from water where we take bath."

"I reckon we'd better look for 'em," he said. "You'll have to ride in front of me on my horse."

She nodded that she understood. Again wiping blood from her mouth and nose, she walked over to the Palouse and swung up on its back, using only the saddlehorn as if the stirrups were not needed.

"I'll take you to the doctor at Fort Sill," he said as he put his foot in the left stirrup. "You've had some mighty rough treatment."

"No go to *Tosi Tivo* medicine man," she said, as he swung his leg over the stud's rump, settling in behind her with the reins in his left hand.

"You're hurt. Those bruises need attention."

"No go," she said emphatically.

He turned the Palouse north, keeping it at a walk when they left the clearing. Slocum was careful not to put his free hand on her waist to keep her in the saddle. He remembered what Major Thompson had said about Senatey hating all white men.

"Show me where the soldiers found you when you were taking your bath," he said. "I'm hoping the same thing that happened to you isn't happening to the other women. There could be big trouble on the reservation if Conas finds out what was done to his women, and in particular what they did to you. Major Thompson isn't gonna be happy. He could have a Comanche uprising on his hands at Fort Sill if any harm has come to the other women. It'll be hard enough to explain what was done to you." He fell silent, figuring Senatey only understood a part of what he was saying. But the truth was, a bloody confrontation between the Kwahadies and Thompson's troops was in the making. Slocum knew the Kwahadie temperment all too well. Conas wouldn't take what had been done to Senatey lying down. He would be after revenge . . . Comanche-style.

"The *Tosi Tivo* soldier chief told me you are the daughter of Lame Bear," he said, after a few miles of silence between them. "I was also told you belong to Quahip."

"Senatey no understand 'belong.' What it mean?"

He had to think about a way to explain it. "He is your uncle, and it is his job to look out for you while your father is in the white man's jail."

"Quahip is brother to my father," she said, as they crossed the prairie.

"The word in English is 'uncle.' Not that it matters. Quahip keeps you safe."

He felt her relax against him a little, but she was still rigid in the saddle, not allowing her back to touch his chest.

"My father is brave warrior. The *Tosi Tivo* treat us like dogs at Stinking Place."

"I saw how bad conditions were. It's a shame to treat men and women of any color that way. Conas told me your children are very hungry. There is nothing to eat but beef with worms in it and moldy flour."

"Many are sick," she said softly. "Many die also. Is wrong to make children die."

"I agree. If I could, I'd feed all the children and the old people myself."

She turned around in the saddle to look at him. When he stared into her deep chocolate eyes he saw her pain and a trace of fear.

"You say good words," she told him. "You no be same as bluecoat *Tosi Tivo*."

"I'm different, I reckon. I was a soldier once, only we wore different uniforms. The white men fought each other in a terrible war. We killed each other. Even back then, it didn't make much sense."

"Why you not same?"

"Can't say as I can explain it. I guess it's because I think a white man doesn't have any more right to this land or any other place than the *Sata Teichas*. Not many white men agree with me on the subject."

"Senatey want to kill *Tosi Tivo* bluecoats. War Chief Quannah say we no make war again. Children die. Old ones die. Is wrong to do this thing."

"We agree on that too," he said. Suddenly Senatey bent forward and began to cough.

Slocum halted the stud when bloody foam came from the girl's mouth, spraying her hands and arms, the pommel of the saddle, and the front of her dress.

"Let's rest a while," he said, dropping to the ground near a thick red oak. Its crimson leaves swirled to the ground in gusts of northerly wind. "You're hurt worse than I thought. If you have blood in your lungs, you'll need a doctor."

She looked down at him from the back of the horse. "Senatey no go to white medicine man," she said, wiping the bloody spittle from her chin defiantly.

"Okay. Just let me help you down so you can rest under this tree for a spell. I'll spread out my bedroll. We can spare a few hours until you feel better."

She coughed violently again, spitting up more pink foam. He reached for her waist without waiting for her reply. After helping her to the ground, he took down his blankets and spread them at the base of the tree.

She gave him a suspicious look and refused to lie down on his bedroll.

"Don't worry, Senatey. I'm not a bad man. I promise I won't hurt you. I've got a little whiskey in my saddlebag. It tastes bad, but it will help with your pain."

"Whis-key is *boisapah*," she said. "Make *Sata Teichas* fall down. No talk. Go to sleep. Bad thing"

"Only if you drink too much of it. I'll just give you a sip or two. You've got my word it won't hurt you."

She walked around him cautiously and settled down on the blankets, holding her ribs as though she was in great pain. "Senatey take only little bit of *boisapah*," she said, slipping very slowly to her knees with her arms still around her ribcage.

Slocum realized that the soldiers had injured her far worse than he'd thought at first. "Lie down and take a swallow or two of the whiskey," he said gently. "I'll tie my horse to that other tree and stand watch so nobody bothers you while you're asleep.''

"No sleep!'' she spat angrily, openly distrustful of him now. "You no stay close. All *Tosi Tivo* bad men.''

It was pointless to argue with her. He took the bottle from his saddlebag, uncorked it, and offered it to her. She took it tentatively, wrinkling her nose at its strong smell. Then she took a very small swallow and gave it back to him.

"No good,'' she said, first leaning back gingerly on her elbows, then resting her body against the tree.

He wouldn't argue with her. He led his Palouse over to another red oak and he tied the reins to a low limb. The girl could have broken ribs or injury to her lungs. He'd seen men die during the war from blood entering the lungs, but that was usually the result of a bullet. He wondered if one of those gutless soldiers might have kicked her during the struggle to get her tied to the tree.

I'll find those three sons of bitches, he thought. I'll be able to recognize them. I'll report what they did to Thompson, but not until after I give them a dose of what they gave her.

He took several pulls at the bottle of whiskey, squatting on his haunches and listening to the wind. Every now and then, he'd glance over to the tree where Senatey rested. Each time, she was watching him. It was painfully clear that she didn't trust him.

A few minutes later, she began to cough again, wincing, gripping her sides, spitting blood.

Damn, he thought. I've got to get her to a doctor, only she says she won't let one examine her. The Comanche medicine man would only treat her with ceremonies and maybe a natural remedy—some plant or root or berry.

Slocum wondered about the other Kwahadie women. If anything had happened to them, a war was in the making and he had the misfortune to be right in the middle of it.

"I should have ridden on with Fannie,'' he muttered, as

if saying it aloud made a difference. He could have taken the hot redhead to the closest railroad line and enjoyed himself along the way, instead of sticking his nose in where it didn't belong. An investigation into the scalping of seven white settlers was a job for the army and the law.

Then again, it was Slocum's nature to take sides when there was trouble. He'd been that way since boyhood. His sense of right and wrong was easily awakened, even when it came to affairs that weren't rightly his. Thinking about it now, with this injured Comanche girl in his charge for the present, he realized that his guns, or his prick, got him into trouble at times. Despite the pleasure that harkening to the needs of his cock frequently gave him, there had been occasional misfires when a beautiful woman had put him in the wrong place at the wrong time. And in this case, it was two beautiful women who were the cause. Fannie had kept him in Cache longer than he had intended to stay, and the lovely Indian maiden was the real reason he had agreed to help track the killers who raided the cabin, so Senatey's people wouldn't be blamed.

He heard her cough again, and now he truly began to worry. If the girl had serious internal injuries, waiting too long to see a doctor would seriously worsen the damage.

He got up slowly, so as not to frighten her, and walked over to the tree where she lay. "More blood," he said darkly. "I want you to try to trust me, Senatey. I know you don't trust white men, but I'm asking you to make an exception . . . to believe my words when I say it is very important to get you to a doctor." As he said this, he used sign language to help her understand, but he wasn't quite sure of some of the signs.

"No," she said, shaking her head. "No go to white medicine man at Stinking Place."

"You could die, Senatey. You are bleeding inside."

"No go," she said again, but as she spoke a trace of a tear appeared in the corner of each eye.

"You're in a lot of pain. The white doctor can give you something for it, so it won't hurt so bad."

"No!" she said, more emphatically this time.

Slocum looked up at the sky, feeling helpless. He wouldn't force her to go. "I speak true words when I tell you I am not a bad man like the other white men you've known. You can trust me. I won't let anything happen to you if you let me take you back to the fort to see the doctor. I'll stay right there with you the whole time, to make sure nothing bad happens."

She was watching him closely as he spoke. "You not same. I see in eyes. Hear in words."

"Then I want you to trust me. The white doctor at the fort can help you."

"No," Senatey said, but there was less anger in her voice now. "I hear what you say. I *Sata Teichas*. No *Tosi Tivo*. Isa Tai give me help. No see white medicine man."

"Isa Tai is your tribal medicine man?" He gave the sign for someone who heals sickness.

She nodded and then suddenly coughed again. Pink foam sprayed from her lips in spite of her efforts to keep them closed, adding to the blood covering the front of her dress.

Slocum spread his hands in a helpless gesture. "Can't you see how bad it is? You are bleeding inside. You've got to have some medical attention."

Before he got everything said, her head fell back against the tree and her eyes closed. Her arms dropped limply on the ground beside her. She was unconscious.

"That does it," Slocum muttered, wheeling for his horse. His mind was made up. He was taking her to the post surgeon at Fort Sill whether she liked it or not. The responsibility was his now to make certain she was given proper medical treatment. No doubt she would be angry, but that seemed less important than saving her life.

He led over the stud and left it ground-hitched while he bent down to lift her in his arms with his blankets wrapped around her. It was a struggle, but he mounted his horse with the girl cradled in the crook of his elbows.

Senatey's eyes remained closed as he tried to make her comfortable across his lap, holding her in sidesaddle fashion so that one hand was free to use the reins.

With his beautiful burden resting against his chest, he sent his Palouse due northward, toward Fort Sill, at an easy walk to keep from jarring her any more than necessary. From the first time he saw Senatey, he'd wanted to hold her in his arms, but not like this, with her life hanging in the balance.

9

Senatey lay unconscious in his arms, groaning every now and then when the Palouse crossed rough ground. Slocum angled north and west across empty land that had once been the prime hunting ground for the Arapaho and Kiowa tribes. But now the buffalo were gone, killed off by hide hunters who slaughtered the animals just for their furry skins. Mounds of sun-bleached buffalo bones lay in the clumps of late fall grasses, proof that this was once one of the most fertile hunting lands in the Indian Nations.

He came to a creek and his Palouse snorted a warning. He pulled back on the reins, trying to see what worried his horse.

He quickly sighted what the stallion had scented. Lying around a pool where the creek made a bend were the dead carcasses of five Indian ponies.

"The yellow bastards killed their horses," Slocum muttered as he guided the Palouse down to the water. To a man like Slocum, there was something far more tragic about killing a horse than killing a man who needed killing. In a lifetime of being around horses, he'd never seen a horse of any breed that needed anything more than a little discipline—a spur now and then, or the end of his reins across its rump.

As he rode down to the stream, he heard a noise. Out of habit, he reached for his .44.

Off in some bushes to the south of the pool, a human voice cried out softly in pain. He swung his horse in that direction, keeping Senatey close to his chest. Picking his way through scrub brush and slender trees, he soon found the source of the painful moans.

A young Comanche woman lay on her back, her hands and feet tied by ropes to stakes in the ground. She was naked, and it was all too easy to see what had been done to her.

"Damn," Slocum hissed. He halted his stud and climbed down to the ground carefully. He placed Senatey on a patch of soft grass and walked over to the girl.

Blood was oozing from her pubic mound, and a number of deep red marks covered her body. One of her nipples was missing, and he could see tooth marks where someone had bitten it off.

"Somebody oughta cut those bastards' balls off," he said in a savage whisper. He knelt down beside the girl. Her skull had been crushed. A blood-encrusted rock was lying near her.

"Murder," he said. There was nothing he could do for the Comanche girl. Her nostrils flared with slow, irregular breaths. She was dying, and it was clear from her twisted facial features that she was in unbearable pain.

He gave the pool and the bullet-torn Indian ponies a closer examination. Dozens of shod hoofprints were visible in the soft mud around the edges of the pool.

"The sons of bitches won't get away with it," he seethed. "If Major Thompson won't do anything, I'll take it all the way to Washington, to General Crook. He won't want soldiers like this in his army. He's an honorable man, and there isn't a trace of honor in any of this."

It was outright cruelty to leave the Indian woman to die a slow death. He had no choice. There was no way to carry both her and Senatey to the fort. Facing a heartbreaking

choice, he did what he knew he had to do to spare the girl
any more suffering. Taking his bandanna from his neck, he
placed it over her mouth and nose, holding it in place until
her breathing stopped.

When he mounted his Palouse again with Senatey safe
in his arms, his teeth were clenched so tightly his jaws
ached. It had been one of his failings all his adult life, to
get on a mad over something that was none of his affair.
With the bile rising in his throat, he turned his horse back
toward Fort Sill as the sun lowered in the west.

It was a small campfire, flickering in the darkness. As he
rode closer, he heard voices. Laughter, and a few words he
couldn't quite make out. He halted the stud and got down
gingerly with Senatey in his arms. Gently he settled the
blanket-wrapped girl in the darkness under a tall oak.

Walking quietly, Indian-fashion, he approached the fire
with his pistol drawn. He could see the dim outlines of
seven or eight soldiers seated around a firepit. A coffeepot
gave off a wonderful smell.

Slocum crept up to a tree overlooking the camp and
gave each face a close inspection. The men's features were
bathed in dim firelight. His gaze came to rest on a face
he recognized. It was the corporal who had given him
the name Dave Sims back where Slocum found Senatey,
the man he'd given a lesson in fistcuffs when he poleaxed
him in the jaw for failing to show proper respect.

Slocum's temper flared up beyond his control. He knew
this was army business, but his anger got the better of him.
He stepped around the tree into the circle of firelight.

"If it ain't Corporal Dave Sims," he said, "or whatever
your real name is." His gun was aimed at Sims. "You were
supposed to bring me a horse for the girl you had tied up."

All eight soldiers stiffened. Sims gave him a wary look.

"Couldn't find our way back," he said sarcastically.
"Got lost in all them trees."

Slocum kept his gun on the others. He walked up to

Sims, who was drinking coffee from a tin cup.

"You've got a bad sense of direction, don't you, soldierboy?" he said. "My pappy always said one way to teach a mule what you wanted him to learn was to get his full attention beforehand."

With a suddenness Sims didn't expect, Slocum swung the barrel of his Colt across the top of the soldier's skull, sending him spinning away from the fire, his coffee cup flying as he let out a high-pitched yowl.

Sims landed on his chest, rolling, arms and legs askew. As his fellow troopers made moves to jump to their feet to help their fallen comrade, Slocum lowered his gun at them.

"You boys stay real still unless you're ready to meet your Maker," Slocum snarled. "I'll kill the first bastard who reaches for a gun or scratches his ass."

The soldiers froze in their tracks. Sims began moaning in a deep, muffled voice. His hands were pressed over his face and the spot on his temple where Slocum's gun had struck him.

"You ain't fit to call yourselves soldiers," Slocum spat. "I say you're nothing but uniformed chickenshits, to do what you did to those women and those horses. Any sumbitch who don't like being called a chickenshit can call me on it right here and now."

"You wouldn't talk so tough if you wasn't carryin' that gun," a sergeant said from the far side of the fire, his face drawn into hard lines.

"Is that so?" Slocum replied. He walked around behind the others until he came to the sergeant who made the remark. "Stand up, you yellow asshole. I'm gonna put this gun away, and then I'm gonna bust your fuckin' head wide open, just like you did to that Comanche girl I found a few hours ago with her head caved in. Only I promise you I'm gonna do a better job. You won't be layin' there alive, pissing in your pants, calling out to your mamma to come and help you. I'll kill you with my bare hands, and then I'll wire General George Crook about what you did, and what these other yellow sumbitches did to those Indian girls. The ones I don't kill here tonight are gonna face a court-martial, and I'll wager Major Thompson will back me up all the way on this. You yellow motherfuckers ain't soldiers. You're trash, only they put uniforms on trash so you can priss around acting real official. But I'll tell you right now, before we start, them goddamn blue uniforms don't mean a damn thing to me. I never counted 'em, but I'd be close if I guessed I killed four or five hundred men back in the war who were wearin' blue. No reason to stop now, not when I find a few more who are yellow-bellied chickenshits who'll tie down a defenseless woman and bash her skull.''

"Hell, mister, she warn't nothin' but a damn Injun in the first place.'' It was the sergeant who spoke. His muscles tensed and he swung around to make a grab for Slocum's gun hand.

His remark was all it took to send Slocum into action. With all the strength he possessed, he smashed the barrel of his gun down onto the soldier's cavalry hat.

The sergeant groaned and sank to his knees. Slocum quickly turned his Colt on the others. "Any other sumbitch want to give me a try? I warned this fool, and I told him I'd give him a chance to tangle with me without a gun. But he wasn't smart enough. His big mouth and bad intentions got him a split skull.''

The corporal sat up holding his head. He glared across the fire at Slocum. "I'll have you put in the guardhouse for hittin' a member of the United States Army. That's a federal crime, in case you didn't know, mister.''

Slocum's blood was at full boil. He strode back around the fire to Corporal Sims. "If I'm facing charges for one or two counts of striking a so-called member of the U.S. Army, I might as well make it a dozen.''

Before the words had even left his mouth, Slocum swung his gun across the corporal's cheek. This time, the noises of by shattering teeth accompanied Sims's shout of agony.

He fell over on his back groaning, spitting blood and chips of teeth.

But Slocum was nowhere near finished with these men. He took aim at the others. "Every son of a bitch unbuckle your gunbelts and leave 'em right here, 'cept for the loud-mouth who calls himself Sims. We're walkin' back to Fort Sill tonight, only there's one more thing about it you ain't gonna like.

"What's that, mister?" a young private with pink cheeks asked as he began unbuckling his army-issue flap holster.

Slocum chuckled mirthlessly. "You're also gonna pull off your boots."

"Our boots?" another soldier cried. "There ain't nothin' but cactus an' thorns all the way to Cache!"

"Sounds like you've got two choices, soldier. You can show up at the fort a little sore-footed, or you can make me mad. Now, you already seen what I do when I get mad. On top of having sore feet, you'll have a few bumps on your skullbone."

"You're plumb crazy, mister," the sergeant said, sitting up and holding his bleeding head.

"That's what I've been told," Slocum replied, his voice even, emotionless. "My mama used to say I was the cra-ziest child ever raised in Calhoun County, Georgia. Never was anybody in that whole part of the state argued with her. Now get up and take off that gun, or I'll smack around on your head again till you understand I ain't just fooling around."

"What'll we do with our horses?" another soldier asked as his gun and holster fell to the ground.

"You're gonna turn 'em loose. All but one. Get to that picket line and bring me one. Saddle it for me and put a blanket over the saddle. That other Indian girl Corporal Sims and the other two of you tied up is hurt real bad. She's riding back."

"You can't do this to the U.S. Cavalry," the sergeant said as he rose unsteadily to his feet.

"You're dead wrong," Slocum replied. "Because I *am* gonna do it, unless you think you and your soldierboys here are men enough to stop me."

"I'll give the major a full report."

"So will I," Slocum said. "And when I tell him what you did to those women, I expect you'll get to know the insides of that guardhouse real well."

"We didn't do nothin' but fuck a couple of 'em. The rest of 'em run off."

"After you screwed the girl I found earlier, you crushed her skull with a rock. That's murder, Sergeant."

"Not if it's a goddamn Injun it ain't."

"Another lesson you've got coming, soldierboy. Indians are people. And to tell you the truth, shithead, I'd rather know just about any kind of Indian than know any more about you than I already do. You're a yellow chickenshit hiding behind a uniform, and the same goes for the rest of you who took any part in what happened to those Comanche girls."

"I'll go get that horse," the private said, walking away from the fire with his head lowered.

Slocum addressed the others. "Start pulling off those cavalry boots, boys. If they ain't off by the time I count to ten, I'll start shootin' holes in their soles while your feet are still in 'em."

In dead silence, the dejected soldiers began pulling off their high-topped boots in the firelight. One man muttered, "I'll be a cripple the rest of my life by the time I get through pickin' all the cactus thorns outa my feet."

Slocum kept a keen eye on the seven men while he listened for the return of the private with a saddled horse. Moments later, after the last soldier was in his stocking feet, Slocum heard hooves coming through the darkness at a walk.

"All saddled up an' ready, mister," the private said, handing Slocum the reins on a sorrel gelding.

"Get your boots off," Slocum snapped. He turned to the

rest of the soldiers. "You boys start walking toward Fort Still. I'll be right behind you. The first son of a bitch who tries to double back to catch one of those loose horses is gonna get shot for his trouble."

The eight uniformed men took mincing steps away from the firepit without their weapons or boots, soon disappearing into the dark. Only then did Slocum's rage begin to cool. There was more important business at hand. He had to get Senatey to the post surgeon before the blood in her lungs killed her.

10

He piled the troopers' boots onto the campfire and stood there for a few moments watching them burn. Then he picked up their pistol belts and tossed them into the dark brush. Next he tossed their Remington army-issue rifles out of sight behind the bushes and trees.

In a ravine only a few yards from the solders' campsite, he found seven tethered horses. One at a time, he turned them loose to wander and graze, waving his arms in the air to send them southward, away from the march of the boot-less soldiers.

Satisfied that he'd done all he could to keep the troopers afoot, he returned to Senatey, leading the sorrel cavalry horse. She was still unconscious. It would take precious time to fashion a travois from cut poles with his blankets stretched between them. By the blood on the front of her dress he guessed time was running short for the Comanche girl.

He tied the cavalry animal to his saddlehorn and gently lifted Senatey in his arms. In the starlight he saw her eyelids flutter once, but she slipped back into unconsciousness as he mounted the Palouse.

He'd made up his mind, regardless of the girl's wishes.

He was taking her to the post doctor. Her injuries were too severe to leave him any other choice.

Traveling by starlight, he headed toward the fort with the girl nestled against him.

False dawn grayed the eastern skies as he rode slowly through the gates of the fort. He could hear the dogs barking at his approach. The sentries gave him curious stares when they saw the Comanche woman in his arms, but they waved him through as if he were a familiar figure at Fort Sill.

He guided his stud to the post hospital. An orderly half-asleep on a wooden bench stumbled to his feet, blinking in the haze of the pale light.

"What's the post surgeon's name?" Slocum asked as he brought his horse to a halt at the hitchrail.

"Major Green, sir."

Slocum stepped gingerly to the ground with his lovely burden balanced in one arm. "Get him for me. This girl needs medical attention right away."

The orderly blinked. "But she's an Indian. Doc Green don't work on sick Indians."

"He's gonna work on this one."

"Pardon me fer sayin' it, sir, but you ain't no officer an' no civilian is gonna tell Doc Green what to do. Besides, he's asleep."

"Then wake him up, soldier, and do it real quick before I lose my temper."

"It's against orders, sir."

"I'm giving you new orders."

"But you ain't a soldier, if you'll pardon me makin' the observation."

"Wake him up anyway," Slocum demanded, carrying Senatey up the steps. "This woman was almost killed by three of your goddamn soldiers, and I assure you Major Thompson will give Doc Green the authority to work on her. Otherwise, I'll be forced to send General George

Crook, a personal friend of mine, a telegram explaining how you and Doc Green and everybody else on this military post refused to help an injured woman.''

''Doc ain't gonna like it,'' the orderly objected. But as he said it, he started toward the darkened barracks across the parade ground.

''I don't remember asking you if he'd like it, soldier. I said to wake him up and get him over here.''

Horace Green bent over Senatey in the light cast by a coal oil lantern next to the bed where she lay. Despite what the orderly said, Major Green seemed willing enough to examine the girl after Slocum told him about the nature and cause of her injuries.

''She was kicked in the stomach,'' Green said, looking closely at a dark purple bruise below her ribcage. ''Probably ruptured a few blood vessels. May even have caused some damage to the blood vessels in her lungs or throat. You can see the marks here where someone tried to choke her.''

''He gave his name as Corporal Dave Sims.''

''Don't recall a soldier by that name here.''

''I expect he lied to me. He and the other two, a couple of privates, ran off when I asked them to bring me a horse to carry her here. But I found them again. Along with a few more who crushed the skull of another Indian girl after they raped her.''

''Crushed her skull?'' Green asked, peering over the tops of his wire-rimmed spectacles.

''Tied her to stakes buried in the ground. Then they raped her and bashed in the top of her head.''

Green made a face. ''If you can prove that, and you tell our post commander, Major Thompson, about it, those men will be severely punished.''

''I gave 'em a little punishment of my own, Doc. But the army doesn't need men like them.''

"By your Southern drawl I assume you were a Confederate, Mr. Slocum?"

"I was born in Calhoun County, Georgia."

"Whatever side they took in that bloody conflict, men who do this sort of thing to a woman don't deserve to wear a uniform. It's a disgrace to every man who serves honorably."

"We see it the same way, Doc."

Green lifted one of Senatey's eyelids. "She's in a deep coma. Probably the result of shock. I'll give her an injection of morphine for her pain and wrap her ribs. For now, that's about all I can do."

"When she wakes up she'll holler like a stuck pig, Doc. She told me she wouldn't go to a white man's doctor."

Green nodded. "These Indians have their own belief systems, and the Comanches are the hardest to convince when it comes to medicine. They still believe in their medicine men and the old ceremonies."

"I'll appreciate anything you can do for her," Slocum said in a quiet voice. "She's too young to die, and when I saw all that blood coming from her mouth, I knew she needed a real doctor to take care of her."

"I'll do everything I can. Internal injuries are very hard to diagnose."

"I understand. I'm headed over to see Major Thompson, to give him a report of what happened. You can reach me at the Grand Hotel if you need me for anything."

"When she wakes up, if she insists on leaving, there isn't much I can do besides let her go."

"Do as much as you can for her until then, Doc. I'll be back to see how she's doing after I talk to Major Thompson and get a change of clothes at my hotel room."

"Bruce Thompson isn't going to like what you tell him, Mr. Slocum. I assure you of that. The major is a soldier first and foremost. He won't tolerate that kind of behavior from any of the men in his command."

"I'm glad to hear it," Slocum said, turning to leave the

tiny room where Senatey lay. "I would think the Indian agent would be just as upset."

Green gave a humorless chuckle. "Then you don't know Mr. Tatum," he said.

Slocum paused near the door. "What do you mean by that, Doc?"

"George Tatum is about the worst excuse for an Indian agent I've ever run across. He hates all Indians. It's just a nice, comfortable job for him, being Indian agent at Fort Sill. If it were up to him, he'd starve every Indian on this reservation to death."

"I've heard about the wormy beef and the moldy flour."

"It's far worse than that, worse than bad food. I shouldn't be talking about it to a civilian, I don't suppose, but if you hang around Fort Sill any length of time, you'll soon see what I mean."

"Conas, one of the Kwahadie warriors, told me about starving, sick children."

"It runs even deeper. But I'd better keep my mouth shut."

"If, like you say, it's more serious than bad food, why does the army tolerate it?"

Green covered Senatey with a thin bedsheet and turned down the lamp. Then he looked at Slocum. "Crooked politics can run deep into the military, Mr. Slocum. That's about all I'll say in that regard."

"Does Major Thompson know about it? He doesn't seem like the type to tolerate that sort of thing."

"Knowing about it is one thing. Being able to prove it is quite another."

When Slocum realized that the post surgeon was not about to offer any more opinions on the subject, he nodded and left the room.

Crossing the parade ground, he arrived at the headquarters building to ask for Major Thompson just as the sun was rising above the horizon.

"He ain't here, sir," a guard at the door said. "He went

out to look for one of his patrols that was late comin' back to the fort. Someone over at the Indian agent's office said there's going to be big troubles from some of the Comanches here. He rode off last night to check into it.''

Slocum bristled. ''Tell the major John Slocum asked for him. I need to talk to him about the behavior some of his soldiers are guilty of. Tell him I'll be at the Grand Hotel for an hour or two. After I get a bite to eat, I'll be back here.''

''Yessir. I'll tell him. Only, what sort of behavior was you talkin' about that some of his soldiers are guilty of?''

''How does murder sound? Or rape? Killing horses too. Is that enough?''

The private swallowed. ''Are you real sure of that, sir? I don't think any soldier from this fort would commit honest-to-goodness murder or nothin' like that.''

Slocum shook his head. ''I saw it for myself, Private. And I intend to inform Major Thompson as soon as possible.''

''Them's real serious charges . . .''

''You're goddamn right they're serious charges, soldier, and I'll take 'em all the way to Washington if I have to.''

He was bone-weary by the time he got his Palouse stabled at the livery and returned to the hotel. As he started to climb the stairs to his room, the hotel clerk signaled to him.

''There's a red-haired female been askin' 'bout you, if you got back an' all, Mr. Slocum. Said her name was Fannie Brice, an' that you knowed her.''

''I know her,'' he said in a tired voice.

''She wanted me to send our shoeshine boy over to her boarding house soon as you got back, so's she'd know you was okay.''

''No need of that. I'll tell her myself after I get a bit of rest. I just spent a long night in the saddle, and I could use a few hours of shut-eye.''

''She give me two bits to send the shine boy, Mr. Slocum, so I figure I owe her. She said to send the kid over soon as you got back in town."

"I don't suppose it matters," he said, continuing up the stairs.

He was lying in bed naked, almost too tired to move, when a knock came at the door. Slocum sat up quickly and slipped on a pair of pants, wondering if it could be someone from Fort Sill sent by Major Thompson.

When he opened the door he found Fannie standing there.

"I was afraid you'd run out on me," she said, "the way Clyde did."

"I'm not the same type of man as your gambler. Come on in. I'm so tired I can hardly think straight."

Fannie came in and perched on the bed. "Can you tell me what happened?" she asked.

"I found the tracks of the killers just like Major Thompson asked me to," he began, slumping onto the mattress beside her. "I also found two Indian girls, Comanches. One of 'em was nearly dead and the other has serious injuries. I brought her back to the fort to see the doctor. She was unconscious most of the way back."

"What happened to them?" Fannie asked, as she attempted to close the front of her bright yellow dress. Two of its buttons were missing, and a large expanse of her bosom was exposed.

"Some soldiers shot their horses and raped them. They weren't doing anything wrong, just out hunting for game. There's gonna be trouble."

"Trouble?"

"When I tell Major Thompson it was his soldiers who did it to those women."

"Almost everyone in Cache hates the Indians," she said in a distant voice, gazing out his window. "The worst of the lot is that Indian agent, George Tatum. He shouldn't be in charge of any program having to do with Indians. I've met him a few times.''

Slocum's thoughts turned to Tatum. In the back of his mind, he had a dark thought—one that he couldn't tell Major Thompson about until he knew more about Fort Sill's Indian agent and the government contracts for beef.

11

Slocum lay back on the bed. "Right now I'm too tired to think about Indian agents or much of anything else. It was a helluva long ride last night."

Fannie smiled at him. "You need some rest. I can see it in your eyes. Do you mind if I lie down beside you? I have to be at the Wagon Wheel by three."

"Fine with me," he muttered. He was slipping closer into deep sleep. The feather pillow under his head was so soft.

He closed his eyes. The rustle of fabric told him Fannie was undressing, but in his present state, he found he didn't care, even as he recalled the pleasure of the night they spent together.

A moment later, he felt her snuggling against him, all warm flesh and sweet smells. Lilac water and a hint of soap. Then he drifted off into a deep slumber. His final thoughts were on Senatey, her injuries, the blood on the front of her deerskin dress.

He was vaguely aware that he was dreaming, and the dreams were unwanted things, reminders of moments from his past he'd tried to forget.

He saw his father standing beside his mother on the steps

of their cabin in Calhoun County, Georgia. Between them, his older brother leaned against a porch post smiling his roguish smile.

"Where ya been, Johnny?" Robert asked, rolling a piece of straw across his lips.

"Down at the creek . . . fishin'."

"You forgot to tend to them mules," Robert added, enjoying John's swelling misery. He *had* forgotten to unharness the mules before he went fishing.

"I let it slip my mind," he explained. In his dreaming state, as this moment from his boyhood was so vivid, it was as if he were living it all over again.

His father scowled. It was a look John knew all too well. "What if your ma forgot to feed you, son? How'd you feel if I left you tied to a tree wearin' full harness?"

"But I ain't a mule, Pa," John insisted. "Don't see how it's the same."

Pa's frown deepened. "You's sayin' a mule ain't got no feelins? It don't get hungry?"

"I was gonna do it, soon as I got back from fishin'. I swear I was."

Robert grinned so his parents couldn't see it, which only made matters worse. His brother was enjoying his misery more than he should.

"Go fetch them mules," Pa said.

"I'll do it right now," John promised, wheeling away from the porch like the seat of his pants was on fire.

"When you're done, fetch my razor strap off'n the back porch an' bring it to the woodshed," his father added. The remark stopped John in his tracks.

"You mean I'm gonna get a strappin' for leaving those mules tied to that tree? They ain't been there but maybe a couple of hours, Pa."

His pa stepped off the porch, and Robert's smirk widened behind his father's back.

"If a couple of hours don't sound all that long to you, son, then you won't mind a couple of hours in the wood-

shed feelin' the bite of that razor strap.'' He said it without
a trace of humor in his voice, nor was there any twinkle in
his eyes, like there was sometimes on the rare occassions
when he was funning.

"I don't figure I deserve to be punished so hard just for
leaving the mules tied. They was tied in the shade of a
tree,'' he said, backing away as his father approached him.

"Deserve's got nothin' to do with it, son. An animal puts
its trust in the man what keeps it. You done them mules
wrong, an' I intend to give you a reminder of that fact.''

John bowed his head and took off after the mules. But
as he peeked back over his shoulder, could see Robert holding his sides in silent laughter, and that was the moment
when he understood what this strange dream from his child-
hood was really about. . . .

It was after Pickett's charge across the peach orchard, when
the bodies lay like felled trees all around him, that he found
his dead brother. Lieutenant Robert Slocum had been as-
signed as aide-de-camp to General Pickett just weeks before
the battle at Gettysburg, the bloodiest battle of the war. It
was on Little Round Top, where John watched most of the
battle as Pickett's men fired their Brown Bess muskets until
the barrels were glowing-hot.

He hadn't known that Robert was killed by the first vol-
ley of Yankee rifle fire. He had not even guessed that his
brother would be part of the charge—the "highwater
mark" of the Confederacy, as it was called years later. But
he recalled vividly what it was like to find Robert's body.
The pain was like a knife through his heart.

"What's the matter, Slocum?" a Confederate infantry-
man asked when he found John kneeling beside the corpse
of his brother.

"I need a few minutes" was all he could manage to say
as he choked back the tears.

"Hell, boy, there's wounded beggin' fer water an' medical attention all over. Git your ass up an' help them that's still able to use it.''

Slocum whirled. His hand rested on his brother's chest where a minnie ball had pierced his heart. "I'll help soon as I can," he stammered. "This here's my brother.''

The burly sergeant stopped in his tracks. "Sorry, son. I didn't know. Stay as long as you need to. Men'll be along with stretchers after a bit. They'll help you carry him back behind our lines.''

"I don't need any help," Slocum replied, digging into his brother's pocket for a tarnished pocketwatch their father had given him. "He ain't gonna be all that heavy. I'll carry him myself.''

As he lifted Robert off a patch of bloodstained grass, he turned to see what was left of the Confederate lines. For now, the shooting had stopped.

Staggering under the body's dead weight, fighting back tears, he made his way to the hospital tents, leaving his musket behind.

He laid his brother in the shade of an oak tree, filled with emotions he couldn't describe.

"Damn you, Robert! Why'd you have to go and step in front of a musket ball!''

The sound of his voice attracted the notice of a young Confederate captain who was supervising the delivery of bodies into row upon row of dead soldiers.

"What did you say, soldier?" the officer asked, stepping down off his horse as the darkness fell on Gettysburg and the bloody battle scene.

Slocum glanced in the direction of the voice. "Sorry, sir. Just found my brother's body. Wasn't talking to nobody in particular.''

"Is he . . . dead?''

"About as dead as any man could be, sir.''

The captain strolled over, leaving his sweat-soaked horse ground-hitched. He peered down at the body. For a time he seemed at a loss for words.

"A hell of a lot of good men lost their lives out there today, Sergeant," he said.

"Wish it could have spared just this one," Slocum replied with his heart in his throat. He was remembering scenes from their boyhood, despite a desperate wish not to just then.

"These men fought and died for a just cause," the captain continued.

Slocum closed his eyes briefly. "I don't think Bobby ever understood what that cause was, sir. We didn't own any slaves. All that crap about states' rights don't seem to matter much right now."

"It isn't crap, Sergeant. It's a principle. Citizens of a state have the right to determine what is best for the people who live there."

A twinge of anger gripped Slocum's stomach. "What about folks like my brother who don't live in Georgia now? He's gonna be buried here in Gettysburg."

"I understand. You must see it as your brother's sacrifice for those people who still live in Georgia."

"He's dead, so I don't reckon it matters to him."

The captain hesitated. "Do you believe in God, Sergeant?"

"I suppose I do. It's a little harder just now to answer that question with my brother layin' dead here."

"President Jefferson Davis has called this a holy war in which men are asked to give up their lives so others might enjoy freedom."

Slocum wasn't really listening. Staring into his brother's lifeless eyes took his attention from what the captain was saying. "Robert ain't exactly what I'd call free," he said after a bit of thought. "A grave ain't the most free spot to be, in my opinion."

"You'll understand better after the sorrow over your brother's loss passes."

Something turned hard in Slocum's stomach. "It ain't never gonna pass, Captain. He's the only brother I had. I feel like a part of me died with him today at Little Round Top.''

"I'm sure he fought bravely."

"He never was anything else, sir. Bravest man I ever knew, except for our pa. Robert wasn't scared of anything. I reckon he should have been afraid of a minnie ball."

"I'll ask a burial detail to see to the arrangements."

"No need of that," Slocum answered. "To tell the truth, I'd rather see to his burying myself."

"Whose brigade are you with, Sergeant?" the captain asked, after a solemn silence.

"General Thomas Jackson, sir. They call him Stonewall after what happened at Bull Run."

"I'll inform someone with Jackson's brigade that you'll be missing until you attend to your brother's burial. And if you wish, I'll let General Pickett know what happened. What was your brother's full name?"

"Robert Slocum, sir. Lieutenant Robert Slocum."

The captain turned to leave. "I'm sorry about what happened to your brother. We've all lost kinfolks and friends to this damn war. You've got to find a way to put your brother's death behind you. I know it won't be easy."

Slocum used his thumb and forefinger to close Robert's eyelids. There was something chilling about the way he stared blankly at the darkening sky overhead and the dried blood on his lips. "Maybe some can put this sort of thing behind them, Captain. I don't figure I'm the right mix of blood and grit to do it. This is gonna be one hell of a hard day to forget."

"It could just as easily have been you lying there where he is now, Sergeant Slocum."

He felt a tear trickle down one cheek. "To tell it to you straight, sir, I'd just as soon it was me."

In his dream, the surroundings suddenly changed to a quiet place beside the Mississippi River many years after the war, where he studied his reflection on a glassy, sluggish current moving slowly past him. Across a shallow firepit, an old man with tangled white whiskers watched him intently. A Mason Colt conversion was tied to the old man's right leg.

"You gotta let go of the past, Slocum," he said in a voice thick with phlegm. "Grievin' over your dead brother don't do you no good. You let that war turn you hard inside. It's my advice you let go of the memories."

"Some of 'em are damned hard to forget, Colter. I've lost my family. Nothing's left for me back in Georgia. I'm gonna be on the move from now on, till I find a place where I can get some peace."

Colter spat into the fire, chuckling humorlessly and swirling the grounds in his coffee cup. "Peace comes from inside, Slocum. It ain't a piece of ground."

"Something makes me keep looking," he said quietly, with a sweeping gaze toward the western horizon as the sun became an orange ball over a ridge in the distance.

"Hell, that ain't it at all," Colter explained. "Some men are born with wanderlust. You's one of 'em. Trouble is, along with that wanderin' nature, you've taken up the gunfighter's trade fer a profession."

"I'm not a hired gun."

"Don't matter what you call it. When you use a gun against another man, if it's fer pay or over somethin' as simple as choosin' sides, the killin' part is the same."

Slocum thought about it. "If I had to pick the right words to describe it, I reckon I'd say I lost a part of me to that big war."

"Damn near everybody did, son. Hardly anybody got through it without a few scars. Yours run deeper'n most maybe."

He tossed the last of his coffee into the flames and got up stiffly. "Appreciate the Arbuckles, Colter. I'm headed west, up to Colorado Territory. If you're ever in those parts, pay me a call."

"Enjoyed the company, John Slocum," the old man said as Slocum went for his horse. "I'm gonna send a little advice along with you. Remember that when you use them guns you're carryin', the worst reason to take a man's life is over money. Money is a hunk of metal or a piece of paper. A man's flesh an' bone. You spend all your money an' you can always make some more. You take somebody's life, they ain't got but one.''

He awakened slowly, remembering the Comanche girl whose life he had taken last night. Although he hadn't done it with a gun, and the girl was hovering close to death when he found her, his conscience still nagged him. He hoped with all his heart he had done the right thing by ending her suffering. Somehow, what he'd done triggered old memories of Robert and the war, lives lost for no reason he understood back then.

Old Man Colter's advice lingered during his slow period of awakening. When you take someone's life it's the only one they have. The girl had done nothing. She didn't deserve to die.

12

The skies were gray outside his hotel window, a sign of the early winter storm he'd known was coming when he felt the damp chill in the wind as he was riding with Sergeant Watson. Slocum turned his head on the pillow to glance at the woman beside him. Fannie lay there naked, with her hair spread across the pillow like a flaming red torch.

"I've been watching you sleep," she whispered, reaching for his cheek, cupping his chin in her hand. "You must have been dreaming. You kept talking to someone named Robert, and then you said something about a team of mules. I didn't want to wake you."

Slocum gazed at the ceiling. "Robert was my older brother. I have the same dream from time to time."

"He *was* your brother?"

"He was killed in the war. I try not to think about it. Sometimes I dream about him. I reckon it had to do with finding that dying Comanche girl yesterday. I had the other girl across my saddle and she was hurt real bad, so I had to make . . . a choice." To push the scene from his mind, he reached for his father's pocketwatch on the washstand beside the bed. It was a quarter past noon. "I'd best get back to the fort to see if Major Thompson got back and to check on that other Kwahadie girl. She was in pretty bad shape when I took her to the post hospital''

Fannie smiled seductively. ''Have you got time for a little bit of fun?'' she asked. ''It won't take long.'' As she said it, she reached for the crotch of his pants, tweaking his cock playfully.

''I really oughta get going,'' he protested helplessly as the warning swell of an erection began inside his pants leg.

Fannie felt him getting hard and giggled. ''A part of you wants to stay here with me. I can tell. You could stay for a while.''

''I shouldn't,'' he said feebly, making no move to get off the bed while her fingers stroked his prick through his denims. ''I oughta get dressed . . .''

''It won't take but a minute, John,'' she promised, beginning to open the fasteners at the front of his pants. ''You just lie still on your back. I'll show you something else Clyde taught me.''

She drew his cock out and jacked it up and down a few times with her fingers curled around its thick shaft. Then she got up on her knees and straddled him, smiling, looking down at his prick while she guided the head gently into the moist opening between the lips of her cunt.

Slocum looked up at her pendulous breasts and hardening nipples, then the soft lines of her face framed by her thick mane of red hair. ''You're one hell of a beautiful woman, Fannie,'' he said, as she lowered herself lightly onto his cock until she felt resistance. ''It's mighty hard to say no to a request like that.''

''And you are a handsome man, John Slocum, with the biggest prick I've ever seen. I'm still a little sore from the other night, so you'll have to be patient with me. I've got to put it in slowly, and I know you're in a hurry to get back to the fort to look for the Major. Please don't say no to me. Not now, not when I need you.''

''Take your time,'' he told her. The warmth from her cunt was making the head of his cock tingle. He lacked the

resolve at the moment to argue with her. If a beautiful naked woman wanted him to spend a few extra moments with
him while she sat on his prick, it wasn't in him to deny her
request.

"I'd planned to," she replied, with a throaty catch in her
voice.

She pushed more of him inside her, another half inch of
his pulsating thick member. "Oh John," she sighed.

He lifted his buttocks off the mattress to penetrate more
of her. "Relax," he said. "Give yourself time. It won't
hurt but a little while after you've opened up for me." He
knew he should be out at the fort reporting what he'd found
out down at the settlement, but for now he was content to
let passion distract him from his sense of duty.

She stared down at him. "You think I'm a cheap woman
for doing this, don't you?"

"Not at all. I think you're a woman who needs a man
and has been too long without one." The gambler who
abandoned her in Cache must have had higher priorities, he
decided. Or an empty poke that the other woman could fill.

"Just any man wouldn't do," she breathed. Her muscles
were quivering with desire. "It has to be a special man, a
man I want."

"I think I understand." He said it with a mixture of
feelings, spurred on by desire.

"I don't want you to get the wrong impression of me,
that I'd do this sort of thing without really caring about the
man I was with."

He was sure what she said was part truth, part lie. Fannie
wanted to get to San Francisco any way she could. "I
promise you I won't get the wrong impression. I know why
you're doing this. You have ambitions and ambitions are
good. No sense in staying in a place if you can't find what
you want."

She pushed his prick deeper into her dewy mound. A
gasp whispered between her tightly compressed lips despite
her efforts to control it. "I'm glad you understand," she

sighed, wincing slightly when the size of his cock caused her some pain.

"Damn that feels good," he said. Her cunt was so warm and tight, the feeling was lifting him to new heights of pleasure and longing, in spite of his fatigue after a night-long ride with Senatey in his arms.

"I was about to say the same thing," she replied, tightening her vaginal muscles around the hardness of his prick.

"A woman like you needs a lot of loving," he said, rising off the mattress again.

"More than you know," she hissed. She clenched her teeth with building passion, closing her eyelids as a wave of ecstasy spread along the length of her body. "Clyde never understood what a woman wants . . . what she has to have to be satisfied with the man she's with."

It was an absurd question yet he asked it anyway. "Did you love him? Or did you believe you did?"

"He made a lot of promises," Fannie replied as her pelvis ground farther down on his stiff member. "He told me all sorts of things, like how we'd go to California. I guess you could say I loved him, but in a different way . . . not the way I love the feel of your prick inside me."

"I can see to it that you get there," Slocum said as his prick slid slowly deeper into her wetness. "I'll have to send a telegram."

"I believe you, John," Fannie said. "Maybe I shouldn't, but there's something about your face . . ."

"I'm telling you the truth," he answered. "The only way to prove it to you is show you a ticket issued by the Texas & Pacific."

"Will you go with me?"

"I've already told you I have business in Denver. Maybe when I'm done."

"It won't be the same without you," she whispered, suddenly making a face, an expression that was a mixture of intense pain and pleasure.

"You'll enjoy the city. You don't need me to see all the sights."

Now her wet cunt was near the base of his shaft, and she began grinding back and forth, up and down. "It won't be the same," she said again, her eyes tightly shut, a crimson flush darkening her cheeks.

He heard a wet sound as her cunt moved up and down on his member, a sound like the sucking of a windmill sucker rod in the silence of a deserted pasture.

"I'll get there as soon as I can," he promised, wondering, arching his spine to drive his prick deeper into her mound. Was Fannie so good in bed he would travel all the way to the West Coast, to San Francisco, to sample her charms again? It was a hell of a long train ride from Denver.

"Oh that feels so good," she said.

He felt his testicles rising. "Hurry," he responded, his desire heightened by lack of sleep and an urgent need to get to Fort Sill to ask about Senatey's condition. He still couldn't drive the image of the beautiful Comanche girl from his mind, even as Fannie pumped up and down on his prick.

Fannie began slamming her groin into him, but her force was no less than his own as his cock rose to meet her. For a few minutes, they were silent as they sought release, pounding their organs against each other, making the bedsprings groan and squeak.

He caught a glimpsed of her breasts rising and falling with each powerful thrust of her body, their twisted nipples jiggling. In spite of himself, the need for control, his jism came flooding into her pussy in rhythmic bursts.

At almost the same moment, Fannie became rigid and her frantic hunching halted. She trembled slightly, digging her fingernails into his upper arms.

"Yes! Yes!" she cried.

He was lost in his own release for a time and merely let his juices flow.

"Oh yes!" Fannie hissed, her teeth clenched tightly in ecstasy. Drops of perspiration beaded on her skin, her breasts, her stomach and thighs. Shaking, caught in the high point of her climax, it was as if she were encased in a block of ice.

Finally, her thigh muscles relaxed.

His own orgasm ended in shorter, more controlled bursts, and he lay still, panting.

Beyond the open window, a cold wind whipped the curtains away from the windowsill, but neither one of them noticed.

When his breathing slowed, he looked up at her. "*That* was nice, Fannie."

"It was wonderful, John. I don't know how to describe it," she said.

"No need," he told her. "All that matters is we were both satisfied."

She gazed down at him. "It's more than that, John. You do more than just satisfy me."

"Why try to put it into words?"

She let her chin fall, resting it on her chest while she stared down at him. "You're different, John. It isn't just the size of your prick. You give a woman pleasure. I think it's because you're so gentle. You know how to make love to a woman without making her feel used."

"I've never been known for being gentle," he said. A slow smile crossed his face.

"But you are . . . in your own way."

He lifted his head off the pillow and kissed her lightly on the mouth.

Her smile widened. "You see what I mean? You know how to treat a lady. That kiss means as much as anything, when a man feels something . . . after it's over."

"Just a natural reaction."

Her expression changed. "Not with most men. They use a woman and then they can't wait to move on."

He thought about what she said. "It's my nature to move

on to new country, but I try to make a woman feel like the time we spend together means something.''

"It works,'' she said. ''You make me feel like I'm the only woman in the world when I'm in your bed . . . when I'm in your arms like this.''

His mind began to wander back to the fort, to Senatey, and what would happen when she woke up to find herself in the care of a white doctor. ''I enjoy your company, Fannie. You're a great lover. But it's time I got dressed and went out to Fort Sill to talk to Major Thompson.''

"I understand,'' she replied, lifting one magnificent curved thigh, milky, slightly muscled, off his abdomen. There was a sweet sucking sound as his cock was withdrawn from her wet cunt. ''You do what you have to do.''

"I'll try to see you later on tonight.''

She perched on the edge of the mattress. ''I'll be counting on you.''

Slocum rolled to one side and put his feet on the floor. ''I have a sick feeling we're on the verge of an Indian war here in Cache. Those Kwahadies are gonna be blamed for what happened to those settlers down by the Red. I found the tracks of the men who did the killing. It wasn't Indian pony tracks.''

"How can you be so sure?'' Fannie asked as she covered herself with the bedsheet.

"Experience, I reckon. Spent a big part of my life reading hoofprints. Those damn sure weren't Indian ponies that left that settlement. I'm wondering if somebody else could be behind this.''

"But who could it be? Who would kill and cut off the hair of a bunch of farmers like that?''

"That's what I intend to find out, if I can,'' he said as he pulled on his boots.

"But you said you were leaving town today . . .''

He gazed out the window. ''Things have changed. I found a reason to stay a while longer. I want to talk to this

Indian agent by the name of Tatum. Something about this whole affair doesn't add up.''

Fannie gave him a strange look as she rose to put on her dress.

13

Long before he reached the gates of the fort, he could see a beehive of activity. Cavalry troops were forming across the parade ground, sending up swirls of dust into the winds blowing out of the darkening storm clouds.

"Trouble," he muttered, guiding his stud past the armed sentries at the gates. He wondered if Sergeant Watson had located the men who killed the settlers.

As he headed for the post hospital, Slocum told himself that it was none of his concern, that it was army business, despite what he'd told Fannie about looking into his suspicions that the Indian agent, George Tatum, had a stake in what was going on, a profit motive. It was a far-fetched notion but not impossible. Indian troubles in the region around Fort Sill could serve as a distraction from the dishonest dealings of a government agent who was involved in crooked beef contracts, lining his own pockets at government expense.

While it was, admittedly, a stretch of the imagination to think that Tatum was behind the murders down on the Red in some way, it was also clear that the killings and scalpings weren't the work of a Plains Indian tribe who were trying to rid their hunting ground of white settlers but nevertheless left the homesteads standing intact. Scouting for the army had taught Slocum enough about Indian practices to be suspicious of what he'd seen at the settlers' cabins. It simply didn't add up. Scalped women, log cabins left untouched, Senatey's remark about seeing a group of "bad men" she couldn't describe further. It had been enough to prompt Conas to send his women back to the safety of the fort while he and his warriors continued hunting game.

He tied off the Palouse in front of the hospital while observing the rush of activity inside the fort as more and more soldiers formed on the parade ground. Once he learned how Senatey was doing, he needed to find out what all the troop movement was leading up to.

At the far end of a row of empty cots, Slocum saw Major Green giving a soldier some sort of injection. The doctor looked up as Slocum approached.

"Howdy, Major. I thought I'd ask about the Indian girl I brought in."

"She's in that same little room at the back, Mr. Slocum. I have her heavily sedated. Her internal bleeding has slowed down to some extent. She hasn't awakened since you left. The morphine is keeping her asleep."

"You reckon she's gonna be okay?"

Green straightened up. His brow was pinched with thought. "It's very hard to say. Someone gave her a terrible beating."

"Soldiers from this fort. I intend to speak to Major Thompson about it as soon as he returns."

"He's back. A group of escaped Comanches has been cornered by squads of troopers somewhere to the south. Our patrol reported that these were the Indians who murdered those farmers near the river a few days ago."

Slocum frowned. "It's probably a mistake. I expect they found the hunting party led by a warrior named Conas. Those Comanches weren't responsible for the mutilations above the Red. I'd stake my life on it. I found the tracks of those killers for a Sergeant Watson, and I'm positive the prints weren't made by Indian ponies. I've done my share of scouting for the army, and I know the difference. The tracks I found were made by thousand-pound horses, not the little seven- or eight-hundred-pound ponies those Comanches were riding. I'll speak to the Major about it. Might help prevent a war.''

''I fear it's already too late for that, according to what I was told. The Indians are fighting back, and apparently very fiercely at that. It's the reason those squads are forming now. We got a request for reinforcements.''

Slocum shook his head. ''It'd be natural for Kwahadies to fight back if they were attacked. Trouble is, Major Thompson has the wrong bunch cornered.''

Green shrugged. ''I can only suggest that you explain it to our commander, Mr. Slocum. Everything will depend on whether or not he believes you. I was told there were already heavy casualties on both sides. We're preparing for a large number of wounded to arrive at any moment now. Wagons were sent out to bring them back.''

''Sounds like I sure as hell am too late,'' Slocum said. ''If you don't mind, I'd like to look in on the girl. I feel like I owe it to her, on account of what was done to her by those soldiers.''

The doctor nodded. ''If what you say is true, and I don't doubt your word at all, those men should be court-martialed. It disgraces the rest of us who wear these uniforms to have soldiers among us who would do anything so brutal to a woman, regardless of her race. I'm sure you know we have some who feel an Indian isn't quite human. It's a sad state of affairs, but I don't have the authority to change official procedures, and no one can effect a change on the minds of certain types of men.''

''Those weren't men,'' Slocum replied angrily, turning for the room where Senatey was being kept. ''They were cowards.''

Her eyes were closed and her breathing was slow and irregular as her tiny nostrils flared. He leaned over her bunk to get a better look at the bruises on her cheeks and neck. They were worse than when he had seen them in the pale moonlight the night before.

"The yellow bastards," he whispered, unconsciously balling his hands into fists.

The sound of his voice awakened her, and her eyelids fluttered open. For a moment, she stared blankly at the hospital ceiling. Then she slowly became aware of his presence.

He made the sign for true words. "Just wanted to be sure you're okay," he said gently.

The morphine made her words mushy. "This place . . . is white medicine man lodge."

"I had no choice but to bring you here, Senatey. You had to have medical attention."

"Take me . . . Isa Tai. Now."

"I can't do that, not till you're a little stronger. You're bleeding inside. It's serious."

"Take me Isa Tai. This bad . . . place"

Her fear and hatred for white men wouldn't allow her to consider anything else. The morphine was the only thing keeping her from leaving the hospital on her own. "I'll take you to Isa Tai as soon as I can, as soon as you're a little better. Until the bleeding stops you have to stay here. Moving any more than necessary can start the bleeding again."

"No!" she said, wagging her head on the pillow. "Take me now!"

He sat on the edge of her bed. There was a fearful expression on her face, but she was too heavily drugged to pull away. "Listen to my words, daughter of Chief Lame Bear," he began in halting Comanche, a gutteral tongue he hadn't spoken in years. He tried to punctuate everything he said with sign language. "The *Tosi Tivo* soldiers who hurt you are bad men. They will be punished. Not all *Tosi Tivo* are bad. The white doctor here is good. He has a good heart," Slocum continued, stumbling over phrases he could barely recall. "He has medicine that will take your pain away and help stop the blood inside you. I know you don't trust the *Tosi Tivo,* and after what the soldiers did to you, I cannot blame you for feeling this way. But I'm asking you to trust me. I am a friend of Chief Buffalo Hump and Quannah Parker. I was a friend to old Chief Nocona before he died. I have been welcome in the villages of the Kotsoteka, the Yamparika, and the Kwahadie of long ago, before your people were forced to live here on the reservation. I speak true words to you when I say the *Tosi Tivo* medicine man will help you.

"All *Tosi Tivo* speak with the tongue of a snake," she said in Comanche.

"That is not true. There are good *Tosi Tivo.* You must trust me."

She watched him through hooded eyelids but said nothing, as if she might be considering his request.

He kept pressing her, knowing the outcome might save her life. "When the soldiers had you tied to the tree, I sent them away. I stopped them from hurting you. If I was a bad man who was not a friend to all *Sata Teichas,* would I do this?"

Again she remained silent, but behind her dark chocolate eyes he thought he detected a softening of the hard look.

"Trust me just this once, Senatey. Let the *Tosi Tivo* medicine man help you and then I will take you to Isa Tai. I speak only true words."

"I have . . . afraid this place," she mumbled in English.

"There's nothing to be afraid of. The *Tosi Tivo* doctor has a good heart. His medicine will help you."

"Maybe so I stay . . . little time," she answered sleepily.

He knew she was slipping back into unconsciousness. "One more thing, Senatey. Those bad men Conas saw when he sent you back to the reservation . . . what did they look like? Were any of them like *Tosi Tivo*?"

"No be *Tosi Tivo,*" she whispered. "No be same . . ."

"But how?" he asked. "Tell me how they were different, or how they were dressed."

"I stay this place . . . little time," she told him. Her mind was wandering, and she winced as a stabbing pain coursed through her chest.

He was silently thankful when her eyes closed again, even though she hadn't been able to tell him what the "bad men" looked like. She was unconscious. He gazed down at her a moment, struck once more by her rare natural beauty. This woman didn't need lip paint or a fancy dress to catch a man's eyes. But after what had been done to her, she would only hate white men that much more, and with good reason.

"Sleep, pretty lady," he said softly as he made ready to leave the tiny room. "I'll promise you one thing. The sons of bitches who did this to you are gonna answer to me, if the army won't do it. I only gave 'em a little taste of what's in store when I find 'em again."

He strode out of the hospital to find Major Thompson, but he kept an eye out for the soldiers he had encountered the night before. One of them would have a swollen jaw and a lump on his head, but Slocum was on a mad and he intended to add to the list of injuries.

At post headquarters, he was informed that Major Thompson had left with over a hundred cavalrymen for a place called Red Oak Canyon, pulling out two hours earlier. A second detachment of cavalrymen was assembling to follow the major. One of Thompson's aides told him that the Comanches trapped in the canyon were about to feel the swift sword of military justice.

Slocum left the building with a sinking feeling in the pit of his stomach. He was certain that Conas and his hunters were not responsible for what happened at the cabins, yet they were about to be punished for a crime they did not commit.

As he was preparing to mount his Palouse, he saw a cavalryman who looked a little bit like one of the soldiers he'd found at the campfire last night.

Slocum wheeled quickly and trotted over to grab the reins on the cavalryman's bay horse.

"What the hell are you doin', mister?" the soldier demanded as Slocum gave him a closer look.

"Were you one of the men who tied up that Indian girl?" he snapped. He held fast to the reins, but he was still not quite sure enough of his identity, or he would have dragged the soldier out of his the saddle then and there.

"I don't know what you're talkin' about, mister, but if you don't let go of my horse's reins, I'll have you thrown in the guardhouse."

"I think you're one of 'em," Slocum continued, unruffled by the soldier's threat. "Trouble is, I ain't exactly sure. You were sitting at that fire last night, only you weren't the one I swatted on the head."

"You've lost your mind, stranger. I wasn't at no fire last night, but if you don't let go of my horse right this minute, I swear I'm gonna have you arrested."

Because he wasn't entirely sure, Slocum let go of the reins and stepped back out of the way. "If I was certain you were one of 'em, I'd teach you some manners," he warned. "But just in case you do happen to be one of the men who hurt those Comanche girls, I give you my solemn promise you'll regret what you did. I intend to take the matter up with Major Thompson when he gets back, and if that don't work I'll give you a different kind of justice.'

"Are you threatenin' me, mister?"

Slocum gave him a lopsided grin. "It ain't a threat at all, soldierboy. It's a goddamn promise. If you turn out to be one of the yellow bastards who harmed those women, I'll come looking for you, and the whole goddamn United States Army won't be enough to stop me from teaching you a lesson."

"You talk mighty tough. If I wasn't on duty, gettin' ready to ride out of here to kill some Injuns, I'd climb down from this horse an' test you."

Slocum's grin widened. "Any time you feel you're up

to it, soldierboy. Any fuckin' time you've got the nerve.''

The trooper urged his horse away to join a formation on the parade grounds, leaving Slocum standing there trying to cool the rage inside him. It was beginning to seem like men wearing blue uniforms were going to haunt him the rest of his life.

14

As he was riding through the gates, he heard a shout of "Move out!" behind him. Glancing over his shoulder, he saw several columns of mounted troopers leaving the parade ground. At the front of the columns, he recognized the young captain he had ridden up with from Childress.

When Captain Carter saw Slocum, he spurred his horse to a lope to catch up.

"Mr. Slocum!" he cried, riding up beside him a few yards beyond the gates into Fort Sill. "I'd like a few words with you, sir."

Slocum halted his Palouse. "What sort of words?" he said tonelessly.

Carter's pink face turned a deep red. "I'm sure you recall that bunch of Indians we encountered on the way here. As it turns out, you were completely wrong about them. They have been identified as the murderers of those civilians. I let you talk me out of giving the order to open fire on them."

Slocum let out an impatient sigh. "Whoever claims to be able to identify them as the killers is full of shit, Captain. Those Kwahadies were hunting buffalo and deer. They had women with 'em."

Carter stiffened. "You apparently are not the expert on

Comanches you led me to believe you were. At this very hour, Major Thompson has engaged them in a bloody battle. They are not as peaceful as you claimed they were.''

"They're only fighting back. I heard the same report you did, that somebody feels they're responsible for the attack at those cabins. They didn't do it, but if a man shoots at a Kwahadie, he'd better expect to have a heavy dose of return fire.''

"I shouldn't have listened to you, Mr. Slocum. If I had followed my instincts, we would have ended the entire matter right then.''

Slocum nodded, feeling his temper rise again. "I can assure you that you're right, Captain. It would have ended right then and there. You'd be dead as a fence post and so would every man in your command. They'd have killed every last one of you.''

Now Carter's jaw jutted. "You haven't forgotten the war, it would seem. You show nothing but contempt for men in blue. But if your memory any better than your judgment regarding Indians, you will recall who won that war. I've known Southerners like you who can't seem to forget you lost the war. Men like you have a chip on your shoulder.''

Slocum lost control. "It's idiots like you, Carter, who don't seem to be able to forget it. The North won because you had better arms, more money, and more soliders. But like you said, it's over. I'm not the one who can't forget it. As for the chip you say is on my shoulder, feel free to try and knock it off any time.''

"You're an insolent fool, Mr. Slocum. I shouldn't have paid any attention to you when we encountered those savages.''

He gripped his saddlehorn with both hands in an effort to keep from taking a swing at Carter's jaw. "It's the only reason you're still alive, Captain. If you'd have drawn that pistol of yours, you'd be long dead by now.''

"You give those savages far too much respect when it comes to fighting skill . . ."

"That's because I've fought 'em a time or two."

As Carter was about to say more, the columns of troopers came up behind him, swinging southwest out of the fort.

"You're about to see what trained fighting men will do to your Comanches," Carter snapped, lifting his reins as he made ready to ride off.

Slocum grinned. "I sure as hell hope you don't lose your hair while you're at it, Captain," he said, heeling his stud in the direction of Cache.

As the military detachment pulled out of Fort Sill, Slocum thought about the outcome. In one respect, the young captain was probably right. Conas and his hunters would be defeated by the cavalry's superior numbers and repeating weapons. It seemed a terrible waste of human life, that men hunting for meat to feed their starving families would be annihilated over a misunderstanding and someone's failure to follow the hoofprints Slocum found east of the cabins.

Major Thompson had seemed like a reasonable man. Slocum wondered if he stood any chance at all of preventing the deaths of Conas and his warriors. It wasn't really his affair. He knew this. But after he'd ridden no more than a hundred yards from the fort, he suddenly turned his horse and urged the Palouse to a lope, heading south toward Red Oak Canyon.

Slocum heard the distant crackle of gunfire. It was at least a mile away, to the west. He'd passed three wagonloads of wounded on the ride down. As the sun lowered, he judged the fighting would slow down with the coming of darkness, perhaps giving him a chance to talk to Major Thompson about the mistake he was making.

At a crossing over a shallow creek, he saw several cavalrymen riding down to the stream. One was bent over the pommel of his saddle in obvious pain. Another had his right arm in a crudely fashioned sling.

"More casualties," Slocum muttered. He knew the United States Army was in the process of finding out just how hard a small band of Kwahadie Comanches could fight, even with outdated weaponry.

He rode up to the soldiers. One of them spoke.

"I wouldn't ride that way if I was you, mister. There's one hell of a fight with renegade Indians goin' on over that next string of hills."

"Renegade Indians?"

"Yessir. Must be two hundred of 'em."

Slocum remembered that there had been fewer than fifty warriors with Conas that day. "I'm looking for Major Thompson. Tell me where I can find him."

"Right square in the middle of that fight, mister, only you sure as hell don't wanna be no place close to where all that shootin' is goin' on."

Slocum noticed that the soldier bent over his saddle had a very serious belly wound. A man who was gut-shot like that usually died a slow, painful death. "I've got to talk to the major. He has the wrong bunch of Indians cornered."

"The wrong bunch?" the soldier asked. "Hell, there ain't but one missin' from the reservation."

"The men you're fighting were only hunting for meat. It's all a terrible mistake."

He rode his stud across the creek and struck a lope in the direction of the gunfire. He was probably too late to stop a massive slaughter, an unnecessary loss of life on both sides. But what puzzled him most was why Major Thompson would order an attack on Conas and his warriors when Sergeant Watson and his patrol had been shown the right tracks to follow.

The boom of rifle fire grew louder as Slocum neared a box canyon to the west. The sun looked like a fiery red ball hanging above the canyon walls as dusk drew near.

Slocum pulled his stud down to a trot and scanned the trees ahead for soldiers, for now the gunfire was close, only a few hundred yards away.

He saw the wink of a muzzle flash in a stand of oaks east of the mouth of the canyon. The echo of a lone rifle shot filled the forests around him.

They can't even see who they're shooting at, he thought as he turned the Palouse toward the flash of light.

"Hey soldier!" he cried when he came near the oaks, to keep from being shot himself. "Hold your fire a minute! Tell me where I can find Major Thompson!"

A dark figure came around the far side of a tree trunk with a rifle in his hands. "Who are you?" a voice asked.

"I'm the man Major Thompson sent to follow the tracks from the cabins where those settlers were scalped. I need to talk to him as soon as possible."

After a moment of silence, the soldier said, "He'll be off to the south yonder. About a quarter mile. Stay behind these here trees or those goddamn Comanch' will shoot you."

Slocum reined his horse in the direction the soldier was pointing. Off in the distance, an occasional rifle shot broke the deepening silence as dark settled over the land.

"The major's over yonder, mister," a private said when Slocum came to a thicket of slender oaks whose fall leaves were being swept from their limbs by the building winds. "He's real busy right now with them Injuns."

Slocum swung down and tied off his horse to a low limb. "I won't need but a minute, Private. I've got something he needs to hear."

"Watch yer ass," the soldier said as Slocum walked into the trees. "Them goddamn redskins sure as hell got good aim from up on them bluffs."

It came as no surprise that Conas and his warriors were good shots with a rifle. "I'll be careful," he said. He headed for a group of men standing in the shelter of a stand of thick oaks.

"Major Thompson?" he inquired when he came to the edge of the forest.

"Over here. Is that you, Mr. Slocum?"

"It's me," he said, striding to the tree where Thompson was watching the fighting through field glasses. "Apparently you were not successful in picking up the tracks of those murderers after all."

Slocum halted in midstride. "But I did pick them up. I found them east of the two log cabins. I showed Sergeant Watson which way they went."

Thompson took the binoculars from his eyes to stare at Slocum for a moment. "That was not the report I was given, Mr. Slocum. I was told you couldn't find any trace of the killers after a thorough search of the terrain."

"That's a damn lie," Slocum snapped. "Who gave you that bit of information?"

Thompson glanced over his shoulder. "I don't recall the trooper's name. He came to the fort and said you couldn't find anything. Then he reported locating a large group of Comanche renegades in this region."

"Whoever gave you that report is a liar. I showed Sergeant Watson the hoofprints and got him started following them. That's when I found the Indian girls. One of them was almost dead from a head wound she suffered by the hand of some of your soldiers. I took the other one, the survivor, to Major Green. Three more Comanche women are still missing. Some of your troopers found them bathing in a stream and killed their ponies. The two girls I found were badly beaten. One had her skull crushed by a rock. The other was tied to a tree, and three of your soldiers were abusing her."

Thompson frowned. Even in the bad light of sundown, Slocum easily recognized the anger that filled his face. "She was tied to a tree? Exactly what were these men, these soldiers, doing to her?"

"In plain language, Major, it appeared they were about to screw her. The other girl had been raped as well as beaten. She had blood coming from between her legs where they'd used her hard more than once."

"Those are serious charges, Mr. Slocum. What were the names of these men under my command?"

"They gave me names, only I don't think they were real names. But I can damn sure identify them, and so can the Indian girl named Senatey who's at your post hospital now under the care of Major Green."

"It was Chief Lame Bear's daughter?" he asked.

Slocum nodded.

"We could have a major Indian uprising on our hands if Lame Bear hears of this. His people are troublesome to begin with, but if he learns that his daughter was molested, more Comanches will cause trouble. Are you certain of this?"

"I know what I saw, Major. And Major Green can tell you about the extent of the girl's injuries."

Thompson looked up at the canyon. "According to several of my scouts, those are some of Lame Bear's people we have cornered in that canyon. Probably two hundred or so."

"About fifty of 'em," Slocum said. "They were hunting for deer and buffalo for their starving women and children. I told you about 'em when we met the first time."

Thompson frowned again. "What makes you so certain these aren't the same Indians who slaughtered the settlers near the river?"

"Horse tracks," Slocum replied. "Conas and his hunters were riding little Indian ponies, typical of the kind they breed. The horse tracks I found east of those cabins were heavier by several hundred pounds. And there's one more important thing. Senatey told me Conas sent all the women back toward the reservation when they spotted a group of what she could only describe as 'bad men.' She doesn't know the word in English to tell me more about who they were."

"Some of this sounds a bit dubious, Mr. Slocum. However, you do appear to know a great deal about Western Indians. I sent a wire to Washington to inquire about your claim that you served as a scout under General Crook. The return message said your record with the army was exemplary.''

''Stop the fighting here, Major,'' Slocum said. ''You've got the wrong bunch of Indians trapped in that canyon.''

Thompson thought a moment, chewing his bottom lip. ''I'll give the order to cease fire. Then we'll see who gave me that information about the tracks leading here.''

Slocum swept the area with a look of his own. ''I'd like to see Sergeant Watson face to face, while you're at it. He knows I showed him those hoofprints leading east. Somebody in your outfit is a goddamn liar, and I aim to find out who he is.''

15

The soldiers pulled back from their firing positions around the mouth of the canyon as the dusk turned into darkness. Slocum waited with Major Thompson and a squad of men in a dry wash where the troops were being assembled. After sporadic firing, the shooting stopped and an eerie silence fell over the battle scene.

A corporal on a sorrel gelding rode up to salute Major Thompson. "Sergeant Watson ain't here, sir. His company captain said he was followin' some tracks east of here with two squads of cavalry. He ain't reported back since he left the fort."

"Then who brought us the report about following the tracks of these Indians to this canyon?" Thompson asked.

"I believe somebody said it was that Indian agent, George Tatum, sir. I can ask Cap'n Collins. He's the one Tatum told about it."

"Tell your captain I want to see him at once," Thompson snapped.

Slocum rested an elbow on his saddlehorn, listening to the exchange and thinking. His suspicions about Tatum were beginning to seem justified.

After the corporal rode off, Slocum spoke. "I was wondering if the Indian agent might have a motive for wanting

trouble with some of his Indian charges. Conas, the Kwahadie leader of these hunters in the canyon, told me his
people were starving because of rotten meat and moldy
flour. Could be Tatum wanted this to happen, to cover up
some dishonest dealings with beef suppliers and flour mills.
It still don't explain who scalped those folks to get the
trouble started, but it sure as hell wasn't Conas or his hunters. The tracks I found were proof of that. Maybe Sergeant
Watson will follow 'em out and find out where they take
him. It could give you some answers.''

Thompson appeared to be considering what Slocum said.
''I know Tatum can be a surly sort, but I never thought of
him as being dishonest. I had no reason to. The meat is
spoiled most of the time. That part is true, but in summer
heat it's hard to keep meat fresh. Bad meat doesn't nec-
essarily mean he's in some sort of dishonest enterprise with
beef contractors. To tell the truth, Mr. Slocum, I don't think
the government cares all that much about what Indians are
given to eat. Indians are a problem they wish would go
away. I'm sure you're aware that at one time not too long
ago, General Sherman and several other high-ranking officers were in favor of a policy of total extermination for the
Indians.''

''I knew about it,'' Slocum agreed. He looked up at the
canyon before he spoke again. ''Someone has to ride into
that canyon and tell Conas and his men they're free to go.
And you can bet he's got some wounded who'll need medical attention.''

''They'd shoot down anyone who tried to ride in there,''
Thompson said. ''They'll understand when we pull out.
When they see us ride off, they'll know we don't mean to
do them any more harm.''

''They'd still be afraid to go back to the reservation,
unless somebody explains what happened.''

''I can't send any of my men in there. It would be the
same as ordering his execution.''

Slocum took a deep breath. ''I suppose I could do it. I

speak a little Comanche. I only hope he'll listen, that he'll understand this was all a big mistake.''

"If you ride in there, Slocum, you'll be undertaking it entirely on your own," Thompson said warily. "Surely you understand the risks."

"I know the risks real well, Major. I've had plenty of hard experiences with Kwahadies. Conas and his people need to be told they can go back to the reservation without any more trouble. He has to be told about Senatey and the other women. When Lame Bear finds out what happened to his daughter, you can count on having more Comanche problems. These ain't real peaceful people to start with. If Tatum was behind those murders near the Red, maybe that's what he was counting on ... that the Comanches would be blamed and the army would try to punish them, so there'd be a war in the making.''

"It's still only your assumption that Tatum is behind this in some manner," Thompson said. "As military commander of Fort Sill, it's my job to investigate any possible wrongdoing. What you suspect Tatum of doing will be hard to prove ... unless those tracks lead Sergeant Watson to something tangible in the way of evidence."

Slocum tried to listen to the major, but his mind was elsewhere. He was already thinking about how dangerous it would be to try to talk to Conas. None of this was his affair, he told himself. If he had any sense, he'd just keep riding toward Denver.

The soldiers were forming columns east of the dry wash, amid the rattle of curb chains and armament, the click of horseshoes on rock.

"Soon as you pull out, I'll try to ride up to that canyon, Major," he said. "All I'm asking for is your word as an officer that those Indians won't be punished for what happened here. In my book, all they did was try to defend themselves."

"You have my word, Mr. Slocum. No more will be done to them if they return to the reservation peacefully."

"One more thing," Slocum added as he lifted his reins. "I'd like to be able to assure 'em they'll get at least one good ration of beef and flour for every man, woman, and child after they go back."

"That doesn't seem too much to ask. I know conditions are deplorable at times. I'll make sure they get good meat and flour upon their return. I'll see to it personally."

Slocum turned his horse toward the mouth of the canyon. "I'll tell Conas what you said, Major. Now all I've gotta do is hope he'll believe me."

He rode out of the wash, through deep oak forests, onto the edge of a broad grassy plain. Looping the reins around his saddlehorn, he began guiding the Palouse with his knees while holding his hands in the air, to prove to the Comanches he was not looking for a fight.

"Habbe weichet!" a voice cried from the darkness near a rock at the base of the canyon wall. It was a warning to go no further unless he was seeking death.

Slocum signaled the stud to halt by swinging his stirrups away from the horse's ribs. He spoke in Comanche. "I want words with Conas. True words. I am a friend."

There was silence and no movement near the rock.

Slocum tried again. "I want true words with Conas. The soldiers are leaving. They will fight the *Sata Teichas* no more at this place."

From the other side of the canyon entrance, another voice said, "I am Conas. Speak, *Tosi Tivo*. I will listen."

Slocum slowly lowered his hands to his saddlehorn, keeping them in plain sight. "The bluecoats know they fought the wrong enemy. They were looking for the men who scalped seven people near the great river, including two women. I told them the *Sata Teichas* do not scalp women, and the bluecoat chief believes me. He has promised not to fight. You will be given good meat and flour when you come back to the reservation, enough for every man and woman and child. The soldier chief speaks true words.''

"All bluecoats speak with the tongue of the snake," Conas snarled.

"Many promises to the *Sata Teichas* have been broken. But this soldier chief will keep his word."

Another silence.

"The daughter of Lame Bear has been injured," Slocum continued. "I took her to the white medicine man, and then I will take her to Isa Tai."

"How was she injured?" Conas asked, his voice thick with anger.

"Some men found your women on their way back to the fort. One of the women is dead." He was afraid to try to explain now that the men were white soldiers.

"There will be war," Conas said. "When these words are given to Lame Bear, there will be war at the Stinking Place."

Slocum knew he had to do some fast thinking and fast talking to avoid angering Conas further. "Senatey told me you saw bad men, that this was the reason the women were sent back. She did not know the word in the white man's tongue to tell me who those men were."

"*Yoh Hobit,*" Conas replied.

Conas was describing dark-skinned men from the south, Mexicans. "The men who hunt for Indian scalps," Slocum said.

"We see them from far away, coming north. Only a few, but with many-shoot guns."

The Comanche hunters had sighted a party of Mexican scalp hunters with Winchester rifles. Now the tracks he found east of the log cabins made sense. "I will tell the soldier chief. He does not know the *Yoh Hobit* were here. The *Sata Teichas* are being blamed for what the *Yoh Hobit* did to the seven *Tosi Tivo* above the river. Now the soldier chief will send his soldiers to look for the *Yoh Hobit*. There will be no more war between the *Sata Teichas* and the soldiers.''

Conas was taking his time before he answered. ''This is for Chief Lame Bear to decide. When he hears what was done to the women and Senatey, he will want war.''

''More of your people will be killed. The bluecoat soldiers are many and the *Sata Teichas* are few. I am a friend to Quannah. I will speak these same words to him. Let there be peace between us. There has been enough war, enough killing.''

Just when it was beginning to seem Conas would not talk any more, he said, ''Tell the soldier chief to keep his word. We will go back to the Stinking Place. Tell the soldier chief to bring meat and flour. Tell him our women and children are hungry. He has seen the worms and smelled our rotten meat. I will only believe he brings us good meat when my eyes see it.''

''He will keep his word,'' Slocum assured him. ''It's the man called Indian agent who gives you bad meat, not the soldier chief you fought today.''

''Man who gives meat is *Mo Pe*.''

Slocum chuckled. ''I will tell the soldier chief you will come back. *Suvate*. Our talk is ended.''

''*Suvate*,'' Conas said.

Slocum turned his horse and rode off at a walk. A slow grin twisted his mouth in spite of the seriousness of the situation he had just been in. The Comanches had given Indian agent George Tatum a name of their own, and from what Slocum had heard about Tatum, the name fit. *Mo Pe* meant ''coyote shit'' in Comanche.

It was past midnight when he returned to Cache. He put his horse away at the livery after stopping off for a few shots of brandy at the Wagon Wheel just before closing time. Fannie almost rushed into his arms when she saw him.

''I've been so worried,'' she said. ''Wounded soldiers have been coming back to the fort all day.''

"It's over for now," he told her, "but the peace may not last very long."

"Would you like some company tonight? I've missed you so terribly, John."

Despite his weariness he agreed to have her come up the back stairs to his room after the Wagon Wheel closed. It was hard to turn down a woman like Fannie.

As he sat on the edge of his bed in the lamplight and sipped from the fresh bottle of brandy he had bought at the saloon, he heard light footsteps in the hallway.

"It's gonna be another long night," he whispered.

He got up slowly and went to the door with the bottle still in his hand, mildly puzzled when Fannie did not knock or ask to be let in. Then a sixth sense suddenly warned him of danger.

Slocum stepped to one side just as the wood of the doorframe splintered. The door exploded inward, driven open by a bulky man in a dark coat and stovepipe boots. He had a pistol in his fist.

As the door and its broken frame fell to the floor with a loud crash, the gunman aimed his revolver at Slocum's empty bed and thumbed back the hammer. He hesitated when he saw that the bed was vacant.

That moment of hesitation was all the time Slocum needed. He clawed his Colt .44 free of its holster and stuck the barrel of the gun into the man's left ear.

"Freeze, shithead, or I'm gonna plaster your brains all over that wall beside you!"

The gunman tensed, rolling his eyes in Slocum's direction as his bearded jaw dropped open.

"You heard what I said, shithead. Be real still, and drop your gun on the floor. If you so much as twitch, I'm gonna decorate this hotel wall with chunks of your head."

"Shit!" the man hissed. He did not move.

"That's right, pardner," Slocum said evenly. "You just shit in your own bowl of soup, and I'm gonna make you eat it. You've got another choice. You can make a play for me with that piece of iron you're carrying, but I'd strongly advise against it. I'm a good shot, but I don't have to be any good with my gun stickin' in your ear. All I gotta do is pull the trigger. I can kill you with my eyes closed if I take the notion.''

16

The bearded giant dropped his gun on the floorboards. "Looks like you got me cold . . . this time," he said. His deep voice was rasping with anger and fear.

Slocum took his pistol barrel from the gunman's ear. "You showed good sense, mister," he said. "Now tell me who you are and why you're here."

"You're stickin' your nose where it don't belong, Slocum. It's the army's affair to track down them murderin' redskins. I came here to make damn sure you stayed out of it. You talked that major into lettin' them Injuns go down at Red Oak, claimin' it wasn't them who took them scalps. I was gonna give you an invitation to leave town an' mind your own goddamn business."

"You meant to kill me. You were aiming for the bed when I caught you off guard. That ain't exactly my idea of a polite invitation to leave town."

"You was mistaken. I was only gonna wake you up an' give you a warnin'."

"That's bullshit, stranger, but right now it don't matter because I've got the drop on you. You didn't answer all of my question. Who the hell are you, and who sent you to deliver this so-called invitation to pull out?"

"I ain't talkin'. You can't prove a goddamn thing on me.

I broke down a door, so I'll pay fer it. I'll swear to the law I stumbled in that dark hallway an' just happened to fall against your door. It'll be your word against mine.''

Slocum gave what might pass for a grin. ''There's two ways it can be your word against mine, asshole. If I shoot you, and show the sheriff this busted door, I'll say I thought you were trying to rob me. It won't matter what you have to say about it, 'cause you'll be dead.''

The man swallowed. He turned his head and gave Slocum a guarded look. ''Sheriff Wall ain't gonna believe no shit like that. He'll see to it that you hang.''

''I'll take my chances . . . unless you start talking, and it had better be the truth. I'm real peculiar about being lied to. If I find out you've lied to me, I'll come looking for you, and the whole Indian Nations won't be big enough for you to hide. Think it over before you let a lie cross your lips.''

In the poor light from the oil lamp, Slocum had only a fraction of a second to see the glint of a knife blade. The giant whirled and swung a Bowie from somewhere inside his coat in a sweeping arc toward Slocum's face.

Slocum took a half step back, just beyond the reach of the deadly blade. He blocked its passage with his forearm, catching his assailant's lightning move with his wrist.

At the same instant, Slocum fired point-blank into the man's chest, but his aim was a bit wide. The crashing blow to his forearm, as the hand wielding the knife struck powerfully just below his elbow, had taken him by surprise.

The thunder of a .44-caliber bullet filled the four walls with a deafening noise. Inside his tiny room, the sound seemed magnified.

Slocum was knocked backward against the wall, but the giant lunged forward again.

''You son of a bitch!'' the bearded assassin snarled, making another swipe with his knife.

Slocum's head bounced off the wallboard behind him. He was momentarily stunned but still able to duck away from the tip of the gleaming blade. It missed his throat by a matter of inches. He felt its breath whisper across his neck.

The giant roared like a mountain cougar when he missed his target again. There was just enough time for Slocum to make a swing of his own with the barrel of his six-gun.

He felt the .44 slam into his attacker's skull. The shock of the blow went all the way to his shoulder.

"Auugh," the giant groaned, staggering back a step or two. His free hand clawed for his cheek where the barrel of the gun struck him. The Bowie knife dropped between his boots with a dull clatter.

It was all the time Slocum needed. It would have been easy to kill the knife-wielding attacker with his pistol, but Slocum wanted information more than he wanted revenge. Who had sent this killer to his room?

Slocum tossed the bottle of brandy onto the bed. He tucked his .44 into his belt, doubled his fists, and lept forward, swinging vicious right hooks and left crosses, slamming his knuckles into the man's face and jaw.

The giant was able to take more punishment than Slocum reckoned. In spite of a series of heavy blows to his head, he staggered but would not go down.

A looping fist came at Slocum's head. He ducked it easily and drove a powerful punch into the man's stomach.

The man groaned and doubled over, offering Slocum the perfect opportunity for an uppercut that, if aimed correctly, would land squarely on the giant's bearded jaw.

With all his might, Slocum brought a driving uppercut from below his waist to the point of the man's chin. The cracking noise that followed could have been either Slocum's knuckles or the jawbone of his midnight intruder.

But following a punch that should have dropped him cold, the huge man shook his head, blinked to clear his addled brain, and rushed forward again.

Slocum came from behind his shoulder with a right hook, employing every ounce of strength he possessed, his feet planted firmly to add his full weight to the blow. He caught the giant just in front of his left ear, a spot that would have rendered any other man unconscious.

The man's knees sagged, yet he would not go down. He wavered, eyelids fluttering. He stared at Slocum through slightly glassy eyes. "You hit like a goddamn mule's kick, only you ain't never tangled with me before."

He charged Slocum once more, windmilling wild punches in a flurry, staggering toward him on unsteady legs.

Slocum had no time to ponder the wisdom of putting his gun away to test the stranger's jaw. He threw a straight right jab at the giant's throat. His knuckles dug deep into the soft flesh and cartilage around the man's windpipe just as a looping left caught Slocum's uplifted forearm.

The giant fell backward, toppling into the washstand where the coal oil lamp stood. Its glass globe shattered, and a ball of flame erupted from the oil spilling onto the floor.

The flash of light blinded Slocum briefly. He shielded his eyes with his hand.

"Holy shit!" a bellowing voice cried amid the sounds of stamping boots.

Slocum drew his arm away in time to see his attacker engulfed in tongues of fire. The legs of his pants turned into torches, and then his shirtfront ignited. He screamed and pawed at his chest as the flames set his beard on fire. Then his tangle of shoulder-length hair crackled with fingers of orange and yellow as the flames surged upward, creating the grisly silhouette of a man standing inside a fireball, pawing feebly to put out the inferno encircling his entire body.

"Help me, you bastard!" the giant shrieked.

The ceramic pitcher of water that had been on the washstand beside the oil lamp lay shattered on the floor, its contents wasted. He jerked the blanket off the bed and tried to toss it over the man's burning body to suffocate the flames.

But just as the blanket fell over him, the giant made a

sudden turn for the open window. Screams of agony erupted from his mouth in rapid bursts. He made a dive for the window, which was one floor above street level, and flew across the windowsill, a burning mass of clothing and flesh and flaming hair and beard. He left a trail of fire and smoke in his wake as he flew headfirst toward the ground.

Slocum rushed to the window as the man hit the ground. Flames licked at every inch of his body, consuming him while he shrieked with pain, kicking wildly and thrashing back and forth in the dirt.

A noise behind Slocum drew his attention from the window. The spilled lamp oil had set one of the walls of his room on fire.

He ran from the window and jerked the sheets off his bed to beat out the flames. Smoke from the burning coal oil burned his eyes and filled his nostrils. Tears ran down his cheeks, and he found it hard to breathe as the combination of smoke and heat singed his lungs.

For several minutes, he ignored the cries coming from the street below, until he put out the fire in his room. The sheets and pieces of peeling wallpaper were still smoldering, but the flames were out and only a few sparks remained.

When he finally looked out the window, he saw only a lump of flaming human tissue and clothing lying just beneath his room at the corner of Main Street and the alleyway that separated the hotel from the other buildings in the business district of Cache.

Close by, he heard someone yell, "Fire! Ring the fire bell an' everybody come a-runnin' to form a bucket brigade!"

Other voices took up the cry at both ends of Main Street. Soon he heard the sounds of running feet. Then, off in the distance, he heard the fire bell.

He turned from the window to make sure the fire in his room was fully extinguished.

"Damn close call," he told himself, inspecting his traveling gear and saddle in the corner of the room. His knuckles throbbed with pain from the blows he'd just delivered to a man who would not go down no matter how hard or in what spot Slocum hit him.

With his eyes still watering from the oil flames, he bent down and picked up the knife. More than a foot of Bowie had come near taking his life, or wounding him seriously. With the knife still in his hand, he went to the doorway to get some fresh air. The knife was the only clue he had as to his attacker's identity now that the flames had consumed the giant's body.

Who would came after him like this? he wondered. What had he done, or uncovered, that was worth killing over? It was someone who knew about events down at Red Oak Canyon. The giant had admitted as much, warning him to stay out of army business.

For the moment, he was unable to think of an answer.

He went downstairs to the hotel lobby, then outside to see what was left of the man who came to kill him.

One thing was abundantly clear. He had stepped on some very powerful toes in Cache—enough to make it worthwhile to silence him.

The giant wasn't an Indian, though he might have expected Indian retribution for bringing Senatey back to the fort in such serious condition. This was something else, with some other motive behind it. The big man had a thick beard, but Indians had little or no facial hair. Slocum supposed he could have been a halfbreed. It had been impossible to get a good look at him in the dim light from the oil lamp. The wick had been turned down low while he was waiting for Fannie.

He walked up to the smoking remains of the body as more than a dozen men continued to pour buckets of water on the remains from nearby water troughs.

An old man in overalls spoke to some of the others standing around him. ''One thing's fer damn sure: This feller's dead as a dead man gits. He ain't nothin' but burnt meat.''

"Who was he?" another man asked.

"Never saw him afore in my life. Big son of a bitch. How in tarnation did he catch hisself on fire like that?"

Slocum, standing away from the group, said nothing. He would give a full report to the sheriff when the time came. Until then, he needed to find out the dead man's name, whom he had worked for, and—more than anything else—the motive that sent him to the second floor of the Grand Hotel bent on ending John Slocum's life.

When it was clear nothing that more could be done, he made a turn for the hotel. He halted in his tracks when he saw a woman running toward him.

Fannie rushed up to him out of breath. "What happened, John? We all heard the fire bell."

"Some guy came to my room with a gun."

"But why? Why would anyone do that?"

"I haven't the slightest idea yet, but I sure as hell aim to find out."

Fannie clasped the front of his shirt. "Let's get out of this town, John. I'll go with you wherever you say. California can wait."

"I'm not leaving till I find out what's behind this, Fannie. I don't take a kindly view of it when somebody tries to kill me. It's just my stubborn nature, I reckon."

"Please, John. Let's go now. Tonight, before anything else happens."

He gave the streets of Cache a glance. "I've got things to attend to first."

She seemed to be avoiding his eyes. "I overheard something at the Wagon Wheel tonight. It may have something to do with what just happened."

"Tell me about it," he said. His words sounded sharper than he had intended. "I want to hear every word."

17

Taking her arm, he escorted Fannie away from the alley, as the odor of burning flesh was replaced by clean night air on a crisp breeze from the north.

"So tell me," he said, when they were well away from the crowd, "what did you overhear?"

Fannie made sure they were alone before she stopped at a dark street corner. "Only a few words. Something about how the Comanche Indians down at Red Oak Canyon got off without a really bad fight because a soldier named Watson rode back to the fort to talk to the Indian agent. The soldiers who were talking about it at the Wagon Wheel acted like they didn't want me to hear what they were saying. They were whispering, and when I came over they stopped talking until I set down their drinks and left the table."

"Sergeant Lee Watson?"

"I don't know. Watson is the only name I heard. One of the soldiers said this Watson wasn't sure what to do, so he came back to ask Tatum how to proceed with something or other. I didn't get all of it."

"Sergeant Watson was in charge of the patrol I sent down the tracks I found near the settlement. I sort of hoped he'd come back with something I could give Major Thompson, some destination for those hoofprints I found east of the cabins where those folks were killed.''

''It seems like Watson needed to talk to George Tatum about what you did. That's all I heard them say before they stopped talking when I brought them their drinks.''

Slocum frowned. ''It's looking more and more like Tatum has some sort of stake in having Conas and his warriors punished for those scalpings. What isn't clear yet is why.''

''Who was the man you threw out your window, John?''

''I didn't throw him out. He jumped when his clothes caught on fire accidentally, after the lamp on the washstand fell on the floor and shattered. He came after me with a gun. I'm sure he was sent to kill me.''

''But why you? What do you have to do with any of this, or the murder of those homesteaders?''

''I ain't got that part figured out yet. What's real clear is that George Tatum is involved somehow. I'm gonna talk to him first thing in the morning. If I had something solid to go on, I'd get him out of bed right now. All I've got at this point is guesswork.''

Fannie placed her palms on his broad shoulders. ''Let's just leave this place,'' she said, a plea in her voice. ''Please take me with you, wherever you plan to go. I promise you I won't get in the way.'' A slow smile crossed her face. ''I'll keep you entertained. Even if I don't get to San Francisco this winter, we'll have some good times together, just you and me.''

He gave it no more than a moment's thought. ''This trouble with the Comanches and the scalpings isn't my affair, but I've had this problem all my life, sticking my nose where it doesn't belong. Those Indians are getting a rough deal, and I'm sure someone wants to see them all killed. Or put in irons. I can't prove it yet, but I think a dishonest Indian agent is behind every bit of this.''

''They're just Indians, John. What could they mean to you? Why are you getting involved?''

''They're human beings, Fannie. We've called them our

enemies for more than a hundred years, when all they wanted was to roam around and live in their traditional homeland where they hunted buffalo and deer for a helluva long time before the white man came. What the government is doing to them now is wrong."

"I don't see what that has to do with you."

"This is my country. I may not be one of its leading citizens, but I know right from wrong. What the army and the Bureau of Indian Affairs is doing to them is cruel. Most folks wouldn't treat a dog the way we're treating reservation Indians at this fort."

"You can't change the whole government's policy toward Indians by yourself, John. Surely you know that. What can one man do? You have no part in what's being done on this reservation."

He turned his gaze toward the reservation. "I understand all that. But I know a few people with influence. I can send off a few telegrams. But first, I need hard evidence of what's going on here."

Fannie was clearly disappointed. "Then we won't be leaving Cache until you do whatever you think you have to do, until you make up your mind or get things changed the way you think they ought to be," she said softly.

"Sorry, pretty lady, but it's just my nature. I reckon I acquired some of it during the war. I saw injustice of every imaginable kind coming from both sides. Never really got over it."

"I suppose I should admire that in you. I haven't known very many men with qualities I admire. Clyde was a card cheat and a thief. It's hard to find anything to admire in any of that."

"Wasn't askin' for your admiration. Just statin' a simple fact."

She tilted her head slightly when she looked up at him. "You're very different from my first impression of you. When we first met, I thought you were a drifter, a horse dealer like you said you were. But you're more than that. Your head is full of unusual ideas.''

"Like I said, I figure it was the war that changed me. I saw more than I wanted . . . more than any man wants to see in his lifetime.''

"And you can't let it go?''

He thought about it. "I still dream about some of the bad parts at night, maybe. I lost my father and a brother to that war, and it still doesn't make any sense. And it wasn't long after that when my ma died of grief.''

"I'm sorry, John. You must want to forget about it.''

"There's some things a man just can't forget, no matter how hard he tries. The war wasn't my fault, and it wasn't my brother's or my pa's. We fought on the side we believed in, and even that wasn't so awful clear. We didn't own any slaves, and a state's rights was something none of us understood, as far as I could tell. We went to war along with our neighbors because it seemed like the only thing we could do, but we were in a fight with folks just like us . . . men who didn't really understand what all the killin' was about. Mostly, I thing we fought it for the politicians. After four years, about the only difference I could see was the color of our uniforms. I killed Union soldiers who were hardly more'n boys, but they were wearing blue and that was all that mattered. Those were our orders, and most of us just followed 'em. I looked down at some of the faces of the boys and men I killed, and I can't forget about it. Same goes for these Comanche Indians. Conas, the leader of that hunting party we met on the way to Cache, said his women and children were hungry, so they left the reservation to hunt for something to eat. That's a *damn* hard thing to forget.''

She lowered her voice and snuggled against his chest. "Not even if I try to help you forget about them?''

He slipped his arms around her waist. "You are a beautiful distraction, Fannie, but that doesn't change a thing. Some son of a bitch is tryin' to blame those Kwahadies for things they didn't do. I can't just turn my back on it.''

"It's the Indian girl, isn't it? You said she was pretty, didn't you?''

"That's only a small part of it. It's what's happening to those starving women and children that sticks in my craw.''

"Maybe I can take your mind off it for a little while— at least until morning?''

Slocum chuckled. "My room is half-burnt. It wouldn't be the most romantic place to spend the rest of the night. These wall and the bed caught fire. It'll stink like the fireplace bellows at a blacksmith's shop till morning.''

"I'll show you another spot, down by the river. I can go to my boarding house and get a quilt. It won't be as soft as a bed, but I might be able to take your mind off things . . . if you want me to.''

He stared down at her. "You can be a most convincing woman when you set your mind to it.''

"Follow me,'' Fannie whispered, taking his hand. "It's a pretty night. A little on the chilly side, but the stars are out.''

"Let me fetch that bottle from my room first. It'll help us stay warm.''

"Get the bottle if you want, John, but I can keep you warm without it. All we need is a blanket.''

"I used mine to toss over that bastard who came up the stairs to kill me. Right now, I wish I hadn't wasted a perfectly good blanket, now you've suggested another way we could use it.''

Her smile broadened. "Never mind suggesting it. Let me show you. Besides, I have blankets up in my room. It won't take but a minute to get one.''

Her enticing smile convinced him. "All right. We'll forget the bottle tonight. I may have broken it during the fight anyway. I'll walk you to your boarding house and stay outside until you bring the blanket out.''

"You won't be disappointed.''

He was grinning from ear to ear as she led him down

the street. "I'm quite sure you won't disappoint me; Fannie."

The quiet riverbank was aglow with starlight. They lay side by side on Fannie's woolen blanket, gazing up at the sky with the sounds of the river and the scent of damp grass all around them.

"You see?" she asked him, after taking a sip of the peach brandy she had removed from a downstairs cupboard at the boarding house while everyone else was asleep. "This is one of the prettiest places in Cache."

"And you're the prettiest girl in Cache," he said, taking a slow sip of the sweet brandy.

She turned on her side. "I know I'm not all that pretty, John, but it's nice of you to say it. We're both alone in a place we'd rather not be in. Somehow, we found each other. If you'll take me with you, wherever you're going, I'll be so glad to leave this town it won't matter."

"I have to go back to Denver, after I ride over to Santa Fe to look at those mares. Business has to come first. If you want company as far as Santa Fe, you're welcome to it. But not until I get to the bottom of this Indian thing. I can't turn my back on it."

"I don't suppose I'll ever understand that part. It has nothing to do with you."

"Maybe," he replied, taking another swallow of brandy, "or maybe I'm here at the right time because I'm supposed to be. I ain't sure I believe all that much in the hand of Fate or Lady Luck, but I won't ride off till I find out why Conas and his warriors are being framed for something I know damned well they didn't do."

Fannie reached for the crotch of his pants. "I've got an idea that might take your mind off it until morning."

"I like the direction your idea seems to be taking us right now," he said.

She stroked his member through his pants leg for a moment, then she stopped. "I'm only asking for one thing from you, John. Take me with you when you're finished with this Indian business. I don't care what direction we go.''

"You've got my promise. I'll either take you with me as far as Santa Fe, or I'll see to it that you get on a train to San Francisco.''

"That makes it sound like there's nothing permanent about our . . . arrangement.''

He looked up at the stars. "A long time ago I gave up on the notion of making permanent plans, Fannie. They never seem to work out.''

"It could be different this time.''

"I can't make a good argument against it, but I know my own nature pretty damn well. Seems like women have a hankering to get settled in a particular spot. Some men just can't do it no matter how hard they try.''

"You're warning me that you'll leave me sooner or later, aren't you?''

He took a slow breath. "I'm only telling you the truth when it comes to me. Don't seem like I'm able to change. Comes a time when I see a new sunrise and I've got to know what's on the other side of the hills where that sun comes up. I can't explain it any better than that.''

"The right woman could make you change your mind, I think, if you gave her a chance.''

"I've tried it a few times. For some reason or other, it just never worked out.''

She nestled her cheek against his neck. "Maybe it's because you've never known a woman like me.''

18

The right woman, Fannie had said. He recalled the only girl he'd known in his life who had seemed like the "right woman" at the time. It was the summer of his fourteenth birthday.

Not far from their Allegheny Mountain home in Calhoun County, Georgia, in an isolated valley at the end of a two-rut road across rough country, John and his brother Robert were fishing in the creek on a sunny spring day. Robert allowed as how he'd had enough of fishing. He took his cane pole and tin of worms and headed back to the house.

John sat on the bank of the creek, alone with his thoughts, until he heard a rustling in the brush nearby. His attention strayed from the cork tied to his fishing line.

He glanced over his shoulder. Melinda Carter, a slender freckle-faced girl from across the ridge to the south, the daughter of a sharecropper family even poorer than the Slocums, came toward him through waist-high thistles and briars.

"Seen you fishin'," she said, smiling.

At fourteen, John didn't care much for girls. He thought about them at night sometimes, but not all that often. "So? How come you sneak up on me like that?"

"Just curious."

"Curious? Ain't you ever seen any fishin' before?"

She came to the spot where he sat with his legs dangling over the stream. She was wearing a dress made of flour sacking and no shoes. "Curious to see what you was doin'."

"I already said I was fishin'. Ain't you got eyes in your head, Melinda?"

She sat down beside him without an invitation. Lately, it seemed her homemade dresses had begun to fill out in certain places. He was vaguely aware of the swell of budding bosoms, a hint of rounding at the tops of her hips.

"I'll tell you what I was really curious about," she said in a soft voice, "but only if you'll swear on a blue robin's egg you won't tell nobody, not even your brother."

He sighed. "How come it's gotta be a secret?"

She looked away. "Cause it's somethin' real personal. If Robert knowed I was interested in . . . somethin' like this he'd tell everybody at the schoolhouse."

"What's so all-fired special about this personal thing you's so curious about?"

Melinda's face turned a deep shade of pink. She waited a moment before she answered him. "It's got to do with what a man an' a woman does in bed at night. Last night, I heard my ma an' pa in the bed, making funny noises. It ain't like I never heard them same noises before, only I never got so curious as I did last night."

"Hell, Melinda, everbody knows what that is. It's called bein' poked, only you're too young to know about stuff like that."

"How come I can't know about it? I'm fourteen, same as you. Ain't that old enough? We're in the same grade at school, so it makes me old enough, an' you know all about bein' poked. I never had nobody tell me about it before."

"Because you're a girl. Girls ain't supposed to know such grown-up things till they're older."

She grinned but still couldn't look at him. Her gaze was

fixed on the opposite creek bank. "I got out of bed real quiet an' I snuck over to their bedroom door. I was afraid I was gonna wake the dog up so's he'd start barkin'. I pushed the door open just a crack."

John waited a few seconds, but when Melinda refused to say any more he asked, "And just what is it you saw that was so damn special?"

"You hadn't oughta be cussin'," she scolded. "What I seen was my ma bein' poked by Pa. He had his tally-whacker stuck up inside her an' she was makin' the aw-fulest noises, like it hurt her somethin' awful."

John wagged his head, disgusted with a girl's logic. "In the first place, it ain't called a 'tallywhacker.' And them noises your ma was makin' wasn't on account of she was hurt. Them's called pokin' sounds."

"Pokin' sounds?"

"The sounds a full-growed woman makes when she's bein' poked by a man. My ma makes 'em all the time."

"All the time? You're joshin' me."

"Not *all* the time. Just at night, when my pa sticks his pecker inside her."

Melinda looked at him for the first time. "It ain't called a 'pecker.' You just made up that name. There's wood-peckers an' such, but that ain't what hangs down between a man's legs."

"How'd you know, Melinda Sue Carter? You don't know shit about bein' poked or nothin' of the kind. It damn sure ain't called a 'tallywhacker,' that's for sure. The right word for it is 'pecker.' I asked Pa one time. He said folks from up north call it a 'cock,' only any fool knows a cock is a rooster. He said it was a pecker an' my pa knows all about peckers and stuff like that."

"It gets hard sometimes," Melinda said, looking off again with a darker color in her face now. "Real hard an' real big. A lot longer'n usual too."

"All girls are dumb," John said, watching his cork

again. "Everybody in Calhoun County knows a pecker gets hard when it's around a woman."

"Does yours ever get that way?" she asked in a timid voice. "I was just wonderin'."

"All the time," John answered, which was nearly the truth. "It's hard as a rock when I wake up in the morning. Same when I go to bed at night."

"Then how come you don't poke somebody so it'll go down some like it's supposed to? Soon as Pa was done pokin' Ma, he took it out an' it hung down like it's supposed to, like when he goes to the outhouse to pee. Looks like if you knowed so much about it you'd poke somebody yourself, if it's like you say, hard all the time."

It was John's turn to blush. "Hadn't found but a few girls I wanted to poke. I've poked more'n my share, maybe, only it has to be a girl I've taken a notion to poke on account of she's so pretty."

"You ain't tellin' the truth. You never poked a girl in your life," she said, sounding sure of it.

"You don't know beans about me, Melinda. I've poked a whole bunch of girls."

"Name just one."

He hung his head, studying his fishing cork with deep intent even though the fish weren't biting. "It ain't right to give off their names. I could if I wanted, but it wouldn't be the right thing to do."

"You're joshin' me again. You never poked a girl."

"Mind your own damn business, Melinda Sue. I said it wasn't proper to tell who they was."

"That's 'cause you ain't never done it."

He glared at her now, embarrassed. "You've never been poked by nobody, so how come you're such a damn expert on it?"

She waited a long time before she answered. "I've been thinkin' how it would feel. Looks like it oughta hurt some, if all tallywhackers get as big an' hard as Pa's does. It sure does look like it'd hurt.''

"You gotta wait till your teats get bigger. Men don't want to poke a girl with little teats. And I just told you it ain't called a 'tallywhacker.' It's a pecker. Peckers don't get hard unless a woman's teats are big.''

"They're gettin' bigger, case you hadn't noticed. I been measurin' 'em with Ma's measurin' tape in her sewin' box.''

He gave her a look of disdain. "They're still too small to make a man's pecker turn hard. Can't hardly notice 'em under that dress.''

Melinda's face was beet-red. "They're bigger'n they look. I'll show 'em to you if you want.''

"I wouldn't be interested in seein' small teats, Melinda. They gotta get bigger 'fore I'd care to see 'em. You ain't old enough yet. Wait a few years and then ask me again.''

"You don't want to see 'em?''

"Not any little ones. A man's pecker don't get hard unless a girl's teats are big . . . bigger'n yours, anyway.''

She turned her back on him, and he wondered if he'd been too tough on her. Melinda was a friend, even if she was a girl with small teats.

"Look, Melinda. You're asking about things that only a full-growed woman needs to know. Wait a spell. What's the big hurry to know all about peckers and bein' poked?''

"Cause I been havin' dreams. I wake up in the middle of the night feelin' real strange. It's kinda hard to talk about. I get this feelin' like I want to know what a tallywhacker feels like inside me.''

"You're too young to be havin' dreams like that.''

"Can't help it, Johnny. I have 'em anyways, an' it seems like they come more regular than they used to.''

John watched his cork idly. The fish weren't biting today, and he was wasting his time fishing. "My pa says it's the devil's work when a boy thinks bad thoughts. Preacher

Barnes always has a sermon against sin real close to Easter. I imagine the same goes for girls.''

"I was only wonderin'.''

John lifted his hook from the water, finding his worm just as it was when he started fishing. "Look, Melinda. I never did mean to hurt your feelings when I said you had little teats. It comes when you get older. My pa's pecker is a helluva lot bigger than mine. Everything grows, like seeds in a garden.''

"They ain't all *that* little,'' she protested. She turned to look at him. "I'll show you my teats if you show me your pecker—or whatever it is you're supposed to call it. That way, we'd know if they was both too small.''

John felt a thickening, a swelling inside his pants. "I'd only do that if you showed me your teats first.''

"How come I gotta be first, Johnny? Looks like if you'd poked as many girls as you say, you wouldn't mind showin' me your pecker.''

"It's account of you're so young.''

"I'm the same age as you.''

He got up slowly, winding his fishing line around the cane pole. "Okay, Melinda. If you promise you won't tell nobody I done this with a girl young as you, I'll take down my pants and show you my pecker. But then you gotta show me those little teats. Won't be fair if I'm the only one who shows what's under my britches.''

"I swear I'll do it.''

He placed his cane pole on the bank and opened the top button of his homespun pants. "If you laugh or tell anybody at school, I'll swear it was all a lie,'' he said.

"I promise I won't laugh an' I sure won't tell a soul,'' she said.

He pulled out his stiffening cock, holding it in the palm of his hand. He was aroused, despite Melinda being only fourteen years old and fully clothed.

"Oh my gosh!'' Melinda gasped. "It's bigger'n my pa's an' his is huge!''

"It ain't even all the way hard yet," John boasted. He could feel it lengthening, throbbing.

"It's real thick too," she said. Her entire face was the color of a sunset. Her eyes locked on his member.

"Now you gotta show me your teats. Remember? You gave me a promise you would."

Melinda stood up and slowly opened the top buttons at the front of her faded dress. As she wriggled it off her shoulders, John couldn't quite believe what he saw. She had rounded bosoms, much larger than her poorly made sack dress suggested. Her nipples were round and pink and hard.

"Maybe they are a little bigger'n I figured," he said, as his cock filled with blood. "It's hard to tell when a dress has got 'em covered." Then Melinda pushed her dress over her hips. She stood naked in front of him. "Don't make fun of me, Johnny. But I wanna see if your pecker will fit inside me the way my pa's fits inside my ma. Maybe this is what Reverend Barnes is always preachin' against on Sunday, only I'd like to see it it's gonna hurt me the way it does Ma."

"It ain't gonna hurt, Melinda, only I ain't all that sure we oughta be doin' this. You'll tell, an' we'll both get in trouble with our folks."

"I done swore I wouldn't. It don't look like it's gonna fit anyhow."

He stepped closer to her. "Lie down in that grass under the shade of that oak tree. We can try it. If it don't fit, then at least we'll know."

She backed away from him until the shade of the leafy oak limbs covered the blush in her cheeks. "Okay, Johnny, but I want you to promise me you won't push it in too deep. An' if it won't fit, you gotta swear you'll quit when I tell you to."

"Lie down," he said. His cock felt as though it was on fire. "I promise I won't hurt you. I'll stop any time you say."

* * *

His pecker did fit, after a bit of work, and thus had begun his first relationship with a girl. Melinda Sue Carter had been his sweetheart for years after that. Until he went off to war.

19

Sheriff Tom Wall gave him a lingering stare. "You're sayin' you didn't know that feller who jumped out your window last night?"

"Never saw him before in my life," Slocum replied.

"An' you're sayin' he came after you with a gun, only you got the drop on him, an' then there was this scuffle, an' he knocked over the lamp?"

"That's what happened, Sheriff. He broke down the door to my room and aimed for the bed with a pistol. I was standing on the other side of the doorway. When he saw the bed was empty, I stuck my Colt against his head. I asked him how come he'd come gunning for me. He said something about me sticking my nose where it didn't belong when it came to those Comanches the army had cornered in Red Oak Canyon. I told him to drop his gun and he did. Then he came at me with a knife hidden inside his coat. I could have killed him with a pistol shot, only I took a swing at him instead. He fell back into the lamp, and that's when the room caught on fire. The coal oil got spilled on his clothes, and I tried to put it out with a blanket. That's when he jumped out the window."

Wall stroked his chin. "I ain't sure I believe you, Mr.

Slocum, but in the absence of any witnesses, I've got no choice but to call it an accident.''

"It wasn't any accident he came to my hotel trying to kill me," Slocum protested.

"Maybe, maybe not. Like I said, I ain't all that sure you're tellin' me the whole truth.''

Slocum did his best to control his anger. "That's my story about how it happened," he said, after a bit.

Wall nodded. The bright sunlight pouring through the window behind him made him look older, exaggerating the deep lines in his face. "Then I reckon that's the end of it. You're free to leave town.''

"I hadn't planned on leaving just yet. I wanted to talk to Major Thompson about a few things.''

The sheriff's face turned hard. "It'd be my advice you leave Cache, before somethin' else happens. Seems you made some enemies.''

Slocum looked past the sheriff at the distant fort. "I never was much good at taking advice, Sheriff, not unless I agreed with it. I'll be staying in town a day or two.''

Wall shrugged. "Suit yourself on it, Slocum. I've got no legal reason to lock you up or run you out of town. But I'm warnin' you. If somethin' like this was to happen again, I'd take a different view of you bein' in Cache.''

Without bothering to reply, he stalked off in the direction of the army post with his mind made up. First, he intended to check on Senatey, then he was going to find out what kind of man George Tatum really was.

She opened her eyes when he came into the room with Major Green.

"How're you feeling, Senatey?" he asked, making signs for the words he used.

"Take me to Isa Tai," she whispered in a dry, thin voice. "No stay at this place.''

"The *Tosi Tivo* doctor says you need rest.''

"Take me to Isa Tai. Sacred chants must be spoken. I will die in this place."

"A white man's medicine can be good," he told her. "It will make you stop hurting."

"My spirit seeks peace," she replied. "Take me to Isa Tai before I die."

Dr. Green spoke. "You won't die, young lady, but you must not move around too much. You have a couple of broken ribs and your internal injuries are still bleeding some."

Senatey looked at Slocum. "What he say?" she asked. He could see the fear behind her eyes.

He spoke to her in Comanche. "To move makes the blood come inside you. It is better to lie down here."

Her eyelids narrowed. "All *Tosi Tivo* lie. Better I go to my people now."

Slocum looked at the doctor. "What will it hurt if I take her where she wants to go in a wagon, an army ambulance?"

"It could cause more internal bleeding," he replied. "It's taking a chance."

Slocum remembered the times he had spent in Comanche villages in the past. "These are superstitious people, Major. They believe in their medicine men. She wants to go to her people. If you'll let me borrow a wagon and a pile of blankets, I'll take her where she wants to go."

"She's not my responsibility anyway, Mr. Slocum. These Indians are charges of the Indian agent and the Bureau of Indian Affairs."

"I'll take the responsibility, Major, if you'll loan me the use of a wagon."

"I'll send someone to harness a team," he said, turning to leave the room.

As the doctor's footsteps faded, Slocum looked down at the girl. "I'll take you to your people, Senatey. We'll carry you to a wagon."

"Now?" she asked. She was not quite sure she believed him.

"As soon as the horses are hitched. Lie still. I'll be back in a few minutes with a couple of men to help me carry ·you on a litter."

Even though she did not fully understand all of what he said, she raised one tiny hand and made a fist over her heart, the sign for true words and a good heart.

He nodded. "I speak true words. I will do as you ask and take you to Isa Tai."

Senatey, in spite of her pain and the effects of the morphine, gave him a smile. One of the most beautiful smiles he'd ever seen in his life.

The Comanche sector of Fort Sill was one of the worst he'd seen. Squalor. Starving women, children, and old men and women watched him drive the covered ambulance across the sections reserved for the Kiowa and the Arapaho. But the Comanches had the worst of things. Open trenches for sewers. Shabbily built barracks with holes in the roof. Everywhere there were signs of neglect, as if the army had decided these people deserved less than any of the other tribes.

He halted the team before an old Indian who stood, with a garden hoe in his hand, blocking the road. Slocum spoke to him in Comanche.

"Point me to the lodge of Isa Tai, the medicine man," he said.

For a long time, the old man did not move. He studied Slocum's face. Then he aimed a crooked finger at a building near the edge of the Comanche part of the reservation. The old Indian had been puzzled when Slocum asked his question in the tongue the old man understood.

Slocum nodded his thanks and shook the reins over the backs of the harness team.

The rattle of the wagon, its wheels, and harness chain drew curious looks from Comanches across the camp. He drove the team to the small building and halted it there. A skinny Indian boy blocked the doorway.

"Help me." Slocum spoke in the boy's native language and used signs to emphasize what he wanted.

The young Indian frowned. "Why should I help a white man?" he asked in heavily accented English.

"Because I have Senatey, daughter of Chief Lame Bear, in the back of this wagon. She seeks the help of Isa Tai."

"You do not speak truth, *Tosi Tivo*. Senatey and four more of our women are dead."

"Can't tell you about three of 'em," he replied, walking to the rear of the ambulance. "One girl was almost dead when I found her. Can't find any trace of the others. But the girl in this wagon is Senatey. Help me carry her inside, or I'll have to do it myself."

Still doubtful, the youth walked over, his thin shoulders nothing but bone and skin, to peer into the wagon. He stood there for a moment.

"It *is* Senatey," he whispered.

In Comanche, Slocum said, "I speak only true words."

The boy looked at him now with a very different expression on his face. "I will help you, but first I must tell the great medicine man to prepare a place for her."

"Do it however you want, only do it in a hurry. This woman has been hurt real bad."

The Comanche ran to the doorway and disappeared inside. Slocum opened the canvas sheet covering the rear entrance of the ambulance to glance inside.

Senatey lay on her back with her eyes closed. Dr. Green had given her another injection of morphine just before they left the post hospital.

"At least she's asleep," he muttered. He was aware that a growing group of curious Comanches were approaching the wagon.

Only seconds later, an old Indian appeared from the building. He was wearing a buffalo skull headdress and held an eagle feather fan in one hand.

In Comanche he said, "The *Tayovises* says you speak our language."

"Not much of it," Slocum replied, "but the boy understood what I wanted. I have the daughter of Chief Lame Bear inside, and she has been asking for you."

The boy came out carrying a buffalo robe. He halted behind the man Slocum believed was Isa Tai, the medicine man of the Comanche tribes.

"Taoyo will help you carry her," Isa Tai said. "Bring her in and put her inside the circle of light."

Slocum had a vague recollection of a ceremony the Nocona Comanches practiced called a Healing Inside the Circle of Light. A dance would begin, accompanied by the slow beat of a ceremonial drum.

"We'll bring her in," he said, climbing into the back of the wagon. "She's asleep. She's been given some medicine to help her with the pain."

"*Tosi Tivo* medicine?" Isa Tai asked warily.

"It was all they had. The doctor at the fort gave it to her before I brought her here."

Isa Tai scowled. "Then the spirit medicine will not work. She will die."

Slocum knew it was senseless to argue with a man who held a powerful position among the Comanches. "It will only keep her in a deep sleep for a short period of time. When she wakes up, you can begin the ceremony inside the circle of light. She asked me to bring her here."

"She will die," Isa Tai said again.

Slocum's patience was wearing thin. "I hope you are wrong, Isa Tai. The girl was sure you could help her."

Isa Tai, aware of the other Comanches listening to what was being said, "Bring her in. If she dies, it will be the fault of the *Tosi Tivo* medicine."

The faded sign above the small log building read BUREAU OF INDIAN AFFAIRS. Slocum went in without knocking.

A gangly man with sandy blond hair and blue eyes

looked up from a stack of papers on his desk. "I didn't hear you knock," he said.

"That's because I didn't," Slocum answered. "I want to talk to George Tatum."

"I'm Tatum. What is it you want to talk to me about that's so goddamn important you can't knock on my office door like a man's supposed to?"

Slocum ambled over to the desk. Tatum was tall and whipcord thin. He had a prominent Adam's apple and narrow, shifty eyes. "Wasn't no sign on this fuckin' door sayin' I was supposed to knock," he replied.

"It's common courtesy."

Slocum rested his hands on his hips. "To tell the truth, Mr. Tatum, I ain't exactly in a courteous mood. But if knocking is so goddamn important to you, I'll knock on your desk instead."

Slocum's remark took Tatum by surprise. He could see it in his face. "I must say you have an arrogance about you. Forget about the knocking and state your reason for being here."

"I'm here to find out why the beef you give these Indians has worms in it, and why the flour is moldy."

"You have been misinformed. Besides, it's none of your business."

Slocum leaned over the desk. He lowered his voice to a chilly whisper. "I'm making it my business, Tatum."

"And what gives you that right?" Tatum said, arching one eyebrow.

"The right of an American citizen to know how a taxpayer's money is bein' spent."

"If you have a complaint, or believe you have one, you can make it through the proper channels."

"I'm damn sure gonna do just that, Tatum," Slocum snarled. "I'm acquainted with General Crook. I used to scout for him and Ranald McKenzie. Unless you give me some straight answers, I'll wire both of them to see if they can explain the rotten meat and bad flour you're handing out here."

20

"I didn't catch your name," Tatum said. He was more wary than before.

"I didn't give you one," Slocum replied. "Not that it matters all that much. I'm John Slocum. I just came from the Comanche sector of this reservation. Can't say as I ever saw anything so filthy in my life. Reminds me of Andersonville during the war. Those Indians are starving."

"I give them the rations required by our treaty, Mr. Slocum. I do not set government policy."

"What you give 'em ain't fit to eat."

"Again, the matter is out of my hands. We are supplied by a contractor. We give the Indians what he brings us."

"Who is this contractor?"

Tatum swallowed, his Adam's apple rising and falling. "His name is Anderson. Bill Anderson."

"Where does this Anderson live?"

"He runs a general merchandise store in Lawton. I believe he owns grazing permits somewhere in the Osage section of the Territory, where he raises the beef he sells us. But as I said before, this is truly none of your affair. If you believe you have a complaint, file it with the government in Washington. I do not set policy. I merely follow it. Now, if you've finished with your groundless accusations, I'm

153

asking you to leave my office. I'm quite busy."

"I'm finished," Slocum said. "At least for now."

He stormed out, slamming the door behind him. At that very moment, he spotted Sergeant Lee Watson riding across the parade ground with four cavalrymen.

"Sergeant Watson!" he shouted. "I'd like a word with you!"

Watson swung his horse and rode toward Slocum with a questioning look on his face. He halted his bay and gazed down from the saddle.

"Those tracks I showed you down at the cabins where those folks are buried," Slocum began. "Where did they take you?"

"They was headed east, toward Lawton, like they was when you found 'em. How come you to ask?"

"Because someone said they led west, to Red Oak Canyon, where a group of Comanche hunters were camped."

Watson nodded. "That's what one of Anderson's boys told us a few hours after you left. We was ridin' along them tracks when a little cowboy named Bob Barlow rode up, sayin' he'd come across the same tracks, an' that they doubled back to the west, an' he'd followed 'em to Red Oak Canyon where this big bunch of redskins was hid out. We turned around an' followed Barlow, to make sure he wasn't seein' things, an' sure enough, there they was, this bunch of Comanches led by this real troublesome redskin by the name of Conas. I sent a messenger to Major Thompson, an' they got 'em surrounded. We rode back here to the fort to get fresh supplies. By the time we got back, the fight was over. Major Thompson said somebody convinced him it was the wrong bunch of redskins."

"Where can I find this Bob Barlow?"

Watson pointed due west. "Prob'ly at Lawton, or out at the Anderson Ranch on Mill Creek north of town. There's usually four or five cowhands at the ranch watchin' over Anderson's herds. He ain't real fond of havin' company out there, so I'd ask in Lawton first so you don't get shot at.''

''Anderson doesn't like having visitors?''

Watson spat off the side of his horse. ''He's a mean-natured cuss, if you ask me, but he's got connections in high places, so he gets the beef contracts for the reservation. Runs a store in Lawton that supplies the other stuff. Flour, dry beans, that sort of thing.''

''The moldy flour.''

Watson hesitated. ''You'd better ask the major 'bout that, Mr. Slocum.''

Slocum made a move toward his horse. ''I think I'll just ride over to the Anderson spread and have a look for myself.''

Once more, Sergeant Watson hesitated. ''Might be a good idea to keep your eyes open. A few of Anderson's boys carry guns. I've heard tell they ain't bashful 'bout takin' a shot at strangers, claimin' they might be cow thieves. This part of the Territory has got its share of rustlers. Sometimes it's the Injuns themselves.''

''I'll be careful,'' Slocum said as he hurried off. Just about everything the Sergeant told him about Bill Anderson made him sound suspicious. It fit the wariness George Tatum had displayed when he gave Slocum little pieces of information about the contracts for food at the reservation.

The land north of Lawton was hilly range country, with a few groves of trees here and there. The Palouse trotted easily over the bunchgrass. The horse was well rested now, and it had been well fed at the livery.

It was getting on toward noon, and as he rode over a rise, a northwesterly breeze brought him a slightly rancid scent, the scent of death.

He halted the stud on a hilltop, trying to trace the smell with his eyes. Off in the distance, he saw a ravine with buzzards circling in the air.

''Wonder what the hell is dead over yonder?'' He re-

called the remark made by Isa Tai. The boy standing guard
outside the shriveled Comanche medicine man's hut had
said that the other three Kwahadie women were dead. Vultures were a signpost that pointed to death. Still, it could
have been a deer, or a rabbit, or some other animal.

He headed the Palouse toward the circling vultures with
a vague feeling that he was onto something and knots in
his stomach. With his heels, he asked the stud for a short
lope. All the while, he was giving the surrounding coun-
tryside a careful examination. Sergeant Watson's warnings
were ringing in his ears. It would be foolhardy to ride into
a trap set by Bill Anderson's rangehands. Watson had said
they were a bit on the trigger-happy side, expecting cattle
rustlers.

On the other side of a wooded hilltop he encountered a
sight he had not expected. There, in a shallow ravine, hundreds of cowhides lay rotting in the sun. Buzzards fed on
the entrails and the bits of skin still attached to the skins.

Slocum sat his horse quietly for a while. He wanted to
make sure no one was around before he urged his horse
down to the ravine. The stench of decaying flesh was over-
powering as he rode down the sloping bank into the dry
ravine.

He swung down and ground-hitched the stud. There were
odd markings on many of the cowhides piled in the draw.
Most of them had different brands cooked into their skin.
Hundreds of hides lay in the bottom of the wash, but it
seemed no two bore exactly the same brand. Some were
Bar B, others Triangle W, and there was an assortment of
markings that were harder to identify because of the dete-
rioration of the hides.

"Stolen cattle," he muttered. Any honest cattleman with
grazing permits on government land would put his own
brand on his beeves. Otherwise ownership would be in dis-
pute come the roundup.

"Anderson is a goddamn cow rustler," he added under
his breath. As he walked among the skins, buzzards circled

overhead and swooped down to feed on the rotting carcasses.

The crack of a distant rifle shot sent him diving for cover behind a tangle of low bushes. The bullet whined overhead, high and wide of its mark.

Slocum had left his rifle booted to his saddle. His only weapons were his Colt .44 and his small-caliber bellygun. He scanned the ridge from which the shot had come from.

Windblown grass, yellowed by the change of seasons, bent in the gusts of air. Slocum couldn't find a shape among the grasses that didn't belong.

Suddenly another gunshot crackled from a grove of slender oak trees, and the blossom of a muzzle flash appeared briefly between the tree trunks. A chuck of molten lead thudded into a stack of rotting cowhides not far away.

This cowboy can't shoot, Slocum thought.

Crouching down and moving slowly to keep from giving his position away, he crept northwest, keeping to the deepest brush with his .44 clutched securely in his fist.

I'll get behind him, Slocum thought, if he doesn't run off before I can find him.

A figure with a Winchester rifle held to his shoulder was hunkered down behind a tree overlooking the ravine. He was a short cowboy with a badly stained felt Stetson. Strapped around his waist he carried a pistol in an oiled cartridge belt. A leather thong tied around his leg held the holster in place.

This fool thinks he's a gunman, Slocum thought as he made a silent approach behind the shooter's back.

When the range for Slocum's .44 was just right, he stood up and aimed for a spot between the shooter's shoulderblades.

"Don't move, cowboy. Drop the rifle and stand up real slow, or I'll blow you to eternity."

He saw the man stiffen.

"How'd you git behind me?" he asked, looking over his

shoulder while clutching the repeating rifle very close to his chest.

"Drop the goddamn rifle," Slocum snapped. "I'm the one who's gonna ask the questions. Don't test me, cowpuncher, or I'll have to prove to you I can't miss at this range. Hell, a blind man could kill you from where I'm standing."

The rifle fell. The cowboy raised his hands.

"Stand up and turn around. If you make a play for that pistol you're wearing, you die same as if you'd swung the rifle on me."

The shooter stood up slowly, his arms held high above his head. He was young, probably twenty-five or so, and all the color had drained from his cheeks.

"I reckon you work for Bill Anderson," Slocum began in a monotone.

The cowboy stared into the muzzle of Slocum's Colt. "Yessir, I do."

"How come you took those shots at me?"

"Them was my orders."

"Most of those cowhides carry different brands. Let me see if I can figure this out without your help. Tell me when I go wrong. Those were stolen beeves, cattle stolen to fill the contract with the Indian reservation over at Fort Sill. You put the hides here while they're still green, waitin' for 'em to dry out enough so's you can burn 'em."

"Are you the law?" the young man asked. His lips quivered as he spoke.

"Right now it don't make any difference who I am. Tell me if I'm right about those cowskins."

"I ain't gonna admit to the part about 'em bein' stole. I'd be askin' to go to jail."

"Would you prefer going to an early grave?"

"You wouldn't just up an' shoot me."

"It'd be my word against yours, and you'd be in a six-foot hole."

"I never stole no cows myself. I'm just a hired hand.

We butchers them steers an' sends the meat over to the fort. Honest, mister, that's all I know.''

"What about the different brands? I think you're lying to me, and I'm liable to shoot you dead on account of it unless I hear something I can believe.''

The cowboy swallowed hard. "Maybe a feller could think they was stole on account of them different brands. Me an' my pardner Barney was wonderin' about it.''

"You work for Anderson?''

"Yessir. He pays real good.''

"Why did you shoot at me just now?''

"We's supposed to keep folks away from this here ravine till the hides git dry enough to burn without makin' too much smoke. A green hide smokes like hell. If'n you didn't know that much already.''

"Where's Bill Anderson?''

"I reckon he's in town, mister. He'll be with Barlow. Bob Barlow is one bad hombre with a gun. If'n I was you, I'd be real careful 'round him.''

"One more very important question, cowboy. If I don't get what I think is a truthful answer, I'm gonna have to kill you and swear you went for that pistol.''

"I sure as hell am gonna tell you the truth if I know it,'' the cowhand stammered.

"Who's in on this at Fort Sill? Who knows the beef they get is stolen?''

"I wish you'd ask me some other question. That one's gonna get me killed if I tell the truth.''

"You'll be dead either way. If you answer me with the truth, I'll give you a chance to get on your horse and ride out of this country.''

For a moment, the cowboy was still. "There's this Indian agent by the name of Tatum. George Tatum. I ain't exactly sure just how he's involved. But he knows this ain't Mr. Anderson's beef we bring him. I've seen Mr. Anderson givin' him money when he didn't think nobody was lookin'. Any fool knows it's supposed to be the other way 'round. When a man sells beef, he gets the money. No reason fer him to be payin' any to the man he's sellin' it to.''

Slocum lowered his pistol a fraction. "Find your horse and clear out of here. If I ever lay eyes on you again, I'm just gonna kill you dead as a fence post without asking any more questions."

"You won't never see me again, mister. I'll promise you that much. This job pays good, but it don't pay enough to be worth dyin' for."

He lowered his hands and took off at a trot, leaving his rifle lying where he dropped it in the grass and fallen leaves.

21

It was a fairly typical ranch for frontier country—a two-room cabin with a dog run, rows of pole corrals, several sheds and barns, a windmill to provide water for its human inhabitants and livestock. Three covered wagons of the Studebaker type were parked in a row behind one of the barns.

That's where they butcher the meat, Slocum thought, taking a closer look at the largest barn from a tree-lined ridge high above the ranch headquarters.

Off in the distance he could see herds of grazing cattle in flat meadows and on grassy hillsides. He pondered why the law, why Sheriff Wall, hadn't visited the place since it was only a few miles, maybe thirty or so, from Cache and less than a dozen miles north of Lawton.

Waiting, watching the ranch for signs of activity, Slocum considered what he already knew. Bill Anderson was supplying the reservation with beef and staples . . . and the beef was stolen, for he had seen proof of it with the branded cowhides. The cowboy who took a shot at him earlier had all but said that the Indian agent, George Tatum, was in on the crooked deal. Now all Slocum had to do was gather enough proof of what was going on to hand it over to someone at the Bureau of Indian Affairs.

"It ain't gonna be easy to prove," he told himself aloud,

still watching the ranch. Where dishonest money was involved, someone usually did a hell of a lot of planning in the event something went wrong. The hides were almost enough proof themselves, but Anderson might have already prepared himself with bills of sale from fictitious owners of the cattle.

After half an hour passed without any sign of movement down at the ranch, Slocum swung his horse to ride among the trees down into a winding ravine that led to a brush-choked arroyo behind one of the cow sheds. What he needed was solid evidence, and this was the place where he'd be most likely to find it.

Stepping softly through patches of dry bunchgrass, he came up to the rear of one of the sheds. He could hear voices inside. It was casual talk . . . laughter, a few words he couldn't quite make out.

Slocum slid over to a corner of the shed and drew his Colt. He stood frozen for a few moments, listening to the conversation inside. The smells of blood and sour meat wafted from a crack in the shed wall.

"Worst job I ever had," someone said.

"Ain't no worse than Folsom prison," another answered over the sounds of a bone saw.

"I did my time in Huntsville. Worst food on earth an' no way to escape work detail. If you lost a goddamn leg, they'd make you carry a shovel out them to fields anyways."

Laughter. "You'd make a pretty sight, Elmer. Hoppin' on one foot to a cotton patch."

"Wasn't nothin' funny about it, Ray. They was goddamn serious 'bout showin' up fer work detail. I had my head busted a time or two when I tried to act like I was sick. A man gets over sickness real quick when his skull's bein' whacked with a damn shotgun butt."

"There ain't a damn thing you can tell me about prison, son. I done my share of time."

The saw went back to work for a few seconds.

"How long did you do in Folsom?"

"Ten of the longest years of my life. A man lays there at night, starin' at that ceiling, wondering if he's ever gonna breathe fresh air again."

"Ten years ain't all that much. I done five at Huntsville an' six more in Fort Smith. You learn to forgit about the years layin' ahead of you inside them fuckin' walls. You do it just one day at a time."

"Easy fer you to say now . . ." The bellow of a cow interrupted the men as a sledgehammer struck a steer's skull. Slocum took a peek through a crack in the boards to see a beeve being felled by a muscular man in leather leggings and a sleeveless shirt drenched in blood.

The steer, with its head resting on wooden stocks, bellowed again and sank to its knees. Blood squirted from a wound between its ears as it fell.

"Wish that coulda been that warden at Folsom," the man said with his teeth clenched. "I used to dream about it at night, what I'd do to him if I got the chance."

"Hell, we all had dreams about breakin' out an' takin' a few of them guards with us. The sumbitches at Huntsville wasn't no damn better."

The man who felled the steer went over to the cow with a knife and slit the cow's throat. "I never heard of no such thing as a good prison," he said, wiping the blade on his pants leg.

"We're liable to get us another stretch if anybody gets wise to what's goin' on here, Ray. Soon as I git me a stake, I'm pullin' out fer Texas. Maybe Mexico."

"Better watch that feller Barlow," Elmer warned. "He's damn sure good with a gun, an' he'll do whatever Anderson tells him to do. He'd as soon shoot a man in the back as sneeze."

Ray opened the stocks and let the dying steer fall on its side. "I wasn't plannin' on sendin' out notices that I aimed to cut an' run, Elmer. One of these days, when I git a few dollars ahead, I'm just gonna disappear.''

"Just make damn sure nobody knows," Elmer said, taking his saw to a beeve's hindquarter on a butcher block. "The less you tell anybody with this outfit, the better off you'll be if you decide to clear out.''

"The only sumbitch I'm worried about is Barlow.''

"You'd be makin' a mistake. Bill Anderson is a tough son of a bitch in his own right. He'll gun you down if you give him half a chance.''

"That's just it," Ray said. "I ain't givin' nobody any kind of notice when I leave. I'll be halfway to the Texas border before they know I'm gone . . . maybe halfway to Mexico.''

"I may not be far behind you," Elmer added. "I hear tell there's some stranger nosin' around, tryin' to pin the blame fer them killins we done down on the Red on somebody besides them Comanches. He could be a U.S. marshal. Hell, he could be damn near anybody. Anderson's worried.''

Ray made a deep cut into the steer's belly and stood back to let the blood flow. "We got protection, Elmer. You worry too goddamn much.''

"That skinny sheriff ain't gonna protect nobody if the shit gets deep, an' I don't trust Tatum no farther than I could toss him into a high wind. A lawman can't be trusted. Sooner you learn that, the less time you'll spend behind bars.''

"It's the money they's after, Elmer. So long as a man is gettin' paid, he ain't gonna say all that much. They could wind up in prison, same as us.''

"I ain't goin' back to prison," Elmer said emphatically, as he trimmed off another section of hindquarter. "I'll die before I spend one more night behind bars lookin' at striped moonlight. I made myself that promise a long time ago.''

"You mean you'd rather be dead than in jail?'' Ray asked.

"Damn right I would. I done spent all the time I'm ever gonna spend in prison. It's the same as bein' dead to some men, an' I'm damn sure one of 'em.''

Slocum crept along behind the barn wall to an open rear door, where piles of intestines drew swarms of blowflies. He'd heard enough of the conversation between Elmer and Ray to convince him. This was an illegal operation, selling stolen beef to the United States government.

He peered around a corner, gun in hand, ready to call for the surrender of both men, when a sound behind him made him whirl around.

A stocky cowboy with a rifle cradled in the crook of his arm came around behind the shed.

"What the hell are you doin' here!" the man demanded, bringing up his rifle.

Slocum had no selection in the matter. It was shoot or be killed. He turned his .44 on the cowboy and said in an even, quiet voice, "Don't bring that gun on me or you'll pay for it with your life."

The rifleman, his face hidden in the shadow below a dark felt hat, continued his motion upward with his Winchester until it was aimed at Slocum.

Slocum triggered off a shot, aiming for the man's belly. A clapping explosion accompanied Slocum's pistol shot.

The cowboy jerked, his body jolted backward by the entry of a lead slug below his breastbone. At the same time, his rifle went off with a booming concussion that seemed to shake the walls of the barn.

"What the fuck was that?" a voice cried from inside.

"A gun, you idiot!" another voice replied. "Run like hell for the bunkhouse so we can git our guns!"

Slocum watched the gunman sink to his knees. There was a strange look on his face, a combination of pain and surprise, as his hat fell off the back of his head.

The sound of running feet alerted Slocum to what was going on inside the barn. He lept to the doorway and aimed his gun into the butchering shed.

Two figures raced out of the front doors. Impossible targets on the move. He made a rush foward along the side of the barn, listening to a groan coming from the man he'd shot at the rear of the shed.

A man ran into view with his head bent forward in a full-tilt charge. Slocum couldn't wait until the man reached his weapon. He took a shot at one of the man's legs. The crack of gunpowder rang in his ears.

The running man collapsed on the hardpan, falling in midstride, howling as he reached for his thigh with both hands.

Suddenly another figure darted out of the shadows beneath the eaves of the barn.

Slocum took careful aim and yelled, "Stop or I'll kill you! You'll never reach the bunkhouse. I've got you square in my sights!"

The man skidded to a halt and looked over his shoulder. When he saw Slocum, his jaw fell open. "Don't shoot me, mister. I ain't the one you're after."

"Depends," Slocum replied casually, freezing his trigger finger before he made a pull.

"Depends on what?" the man stammered.

"On what you tell me. It had damned sure better be the truth."

"I ain't lookin' to die, stranger. Just what is it you need to know?"

"Where's this Bob Barlow?"

"In . . . in town with Mr. Anderson. He don't stay out here all that much. There's this guy who's been nosin' around lately. I reckon that'd be you."

"A pretty good guess. Who else is here? Who's in the ranch house?"

"Jus' Ol' Man Grimes, the cook. A couple of others is out on the ranch some place."

"One of 'em was standin' guard over them green hides, the ones with the different brands."

"That'll be Shorty. Shorty Weeks. He'll come a runnin' soon as he hears them gunshots."

"I've already taken care of him," Slocum replied, taking a quick glance over his shoulder.

"You mean you killed Shorty?"

"I only said I'd taken care of him. He isn't all that good with a gun. I imagine by now he's halfway to Lawton, to tell Anderson and Barlow there's trouble out here at his stolen beef operation."

"How'd you know they was stole?"

"Do I look like a fool?"

"No sir. Wasn't sayin' that at all.

"Just an assumption. All those brands could mean the cows had different owners. If there's a bill of sale for 'em, we've got no problem."

"Maybe there is an' maybe there ain't. I don't know a damn thing, mister."

"That's bullshit and you know it. I overheard what the two of you were saying in the shed a while ago."

Now the wounded man began to writhe on the ground, making sounds of agony. He lay only a few feet from the spot where Slocum had the drop on the other butcher.

"You heard what we said?" the man asked, taking a quick look at his friend. "Then you know he'd rather die than go back to prison."

"The choice is his. If he gets up and wants a little more fight, I'll be glad to oblige him." Slocum aimed for the man's head. "Answer me with the truth. You get just one chance. If I don't hear what I'm expecting to hear, I'm gonna kill you now and swear it was self-defense."

"Honest, stranger, I'll tell you whatever you want to know about anything."

"Is the Indian agent George Tatum in on the stolen cattle operation?"

The butcher rolled his eyes toward the heavens. "He takes money from Mr. Anderson. Honest to God, that's all I know."

"It's enough," Slocum said, lowering his pistol. "Help get your friend on his feet. We're taking a little ride out to the fort, so you can repeat what you just said to Major Thompson."

22

The young butcher named Ray sat a horse in an unnatural way, with his hands glued to the saddlehorn and his eyes turned back toward Slocum as they rode away from the Anderson spread. The ranch cook had given himself up to a rope binding his wrists without a fight, and Elmer, with a bullet wound in his thigh, merely grimaced as Slocum tied the pair to the base of a tree. The rifleman he shot behind the barn died while Slocum was tying up the other two. Ray was all Slocum needed now. He would tell the story of Bill Anderson's crooked dealings to the sheriff and Major Thompson.

But as they were riding away from the ranch with Ray on a borrowed horse, Slocum saw trouble on the skyline. A lone rider was headed into the valley where the Anderson operation sat. Ray stiffened in the saddle when he saw him.

"That's Barlow," Ray said. There was a noticeable change in his demeanor. "You may be wishin' you hadn't showed up here today. Barlow's one bad hombre with a gun."

"I reckon we're about to find out," Slocum replied. He took the hammer thong from his holstered Colt, lifting it a little higher in his cross-pull for a quicker draw. "Could work the other way. Mr. Barlow may be wishing he'd

169

stayed in Lawton, if he's got time to do any wishin'."

"You'd better be fast, stranger."

Slocum watched the horseman start down a grassy slope. He was still a good half mile away. "Bein' fast is a part of it. Hittin' what you aim at is a helluva lot more important when it's over. I've seen plenty of fast-draw artists buried in shallow holes because their eyesight wasn't all it shoulda been. Aimin' true is sometimes better'n bein' fast."

"Barlow's got a bunch of notches in his pistol grips, mister."

"Could mean nothing more than he owns a sharp knife and likes to whittle on walnut handles in his spare time," Slocum answered. He was judging the distance between himself and the approaching gunman.

Barlow slowed his horse, then reined it to a halt as though he sensed something was wrong.

"He's seen you," Ray said. "Now there's gonna be hell to pay, an' I figure you're the one who's gonna be payin' it, sooner or later."

Slocum watched Barlow pull a rifle from a boot below one stirrup leather. "That's what makes a poker game," he said, reaching for his own Winchester. "When the cards get shuffled and the ante money goes down, everybody has reason to think he's gonna be a winner. Then the cards start coming. Dreams die real hard in poker or a gunfight. Some fellers just ain't built the right way, to understand they've got a losin' hand. But when a lead slug passes through 'em, they get a real short glimpse of what it is like to bet it all on a hand that can't win."

Ray glanced over at Slocum. "You sure as hell sound like you know your business, mister."

Slocum flipped his repeating rifle in a road agent's spin to send a load into the firing chamber without taking his eyes off Barlow.

"I missed part of what you said," Slocum told him, his eyelids narrowing in the sun.

"I said it sure does sound like you know you can take

him down. Maybe it's 'cause you ain't never heard of Bob Barlow or his shootin' reputation.''

"I never was inclined to listen to gossip or loose talk," Slocum replied.

"It ain't loose talk, stranger. I seen them notches in the handles of his gun.''

"Notches ain't nothing but notches. Grave markers are what I'd call proof of a man's steady hand.''

"Can't believe you never heard of Bob Barlow," Ray said again, softer this time. He was watching Barlow raise his rifle as the sunlight glinted off its barrel. "He's one of the fastest shootists in Indian Territory . . . maybe this side of the Mississippi River.''

Slocum rested the butt of his Winchester on his thigh, all the while watching Barlow, waiting for his next move. "I try not to listen to things that don't concern me," he said under his breath. "Right now, it's beginning to look like I'm gonna be forced to find out if Barlow is as good as you say he is. Until our business with each other is finished, it's just loose talk and speculation.''

"He'll take a shot at you with his rifle," Ray warned. "If it's all the same to you, I'd like to ride off for a ways, just in case there's a stray bullet.''

Slocum chuckled humorlessly. "If this Barlow is as good as you claim, there's no reason for you to be worried about a shot that goes wide.''

"Just bein' on the safe side," Ray answered back, taking a look uphill at Barlow.

"Stay right where you are or I'll save you all that extra worryin'," Slocum warned. "If you ride any direction besides straight up that hill, I'll kill you. I'm taking you to Major Thompson so you can tell your story about that stolen beef and anything else you know about Bill Anderson's dealings with the army.''

"You wouldn't just shoot an unarmed man," Ray said, sounding sure of it.

Slocum's gaze wandered to Ray a moment. "One way

to find out if I'm bluffing. Turn that horse and try ridin'
off. If you don't hear a gunshot, you can draw two conclu-
sions. One is that you're already dead and a dead man's
ears don't work. Or you can figure I didn't have the nerve
to gun you down. It's like that poker game I was talking
about. You gamble and it can go either way. You win or
you lose.''

Ray passed his tongue across his dry lips. ''I reckon I'll
stay, mister. Can't tell if you're bluffin' or not, but I ain't
looking to occupy no six-foot hole if'n I'm wrong.''

''You made a smart decision,'' Slocum said, heeling his
stud forward at a walk. ''But just so you'll know, I've never
bluffed a man in my life.''

Barlow urged his horse forward, and they rode toward
each other at an almost casual pace, their horse's in a walk.

''I'll hand you one thing, stranger,'' Ray said. His cheeks
lost some of their color. ''You ain't the least bit short when
it comes to nerve.''

Slocum ignored the remark. All his attention was focused
on Barlow, waiting for the moment when the gunman's rifle
barrel tipped down. Even the best marksman would have
difficulty making this sort of shot at long range aboard the
back of a moving horse. If he was any judge of experienced
gunmen, Slocum guessed, Barlow would choose the right
moment to halt his horse suddenly and take aim. All Slocum had to do was to be ready for it, and to be just a
fraction of a second faster when he took his own shot.

''Jesus,'' Ray whispered. His knuckles turned white
where he gripped his saddlehorn. His hands had been bound
together by a piece of rope. ''The two of you are gonna
ride right up to each other before a shot gets fired.''

''He'll pick the time and the place,'' Slocum assured
Ray, as the horses came closer.

''I sure as hell could use a shot of strong whiskey right
about now,'' Ray said. ''I hope like hell Barlow's aim ain't
off to his left by a yard or two.''

''You won't feel a thing,'' Slocum promised, guiding his

Palouse with his knees. "If you catch a bullet from a forty-four Winchester rifle, it'll pass right through you like a dose of castor oil. I've heard some men say it stings a little, but that was just before they died. Maybe the slug won't hit any vital organs. You'll bleed some, but you might live through it. But like I told you before, don't try runnin' out on me when the shootin' starts. If there's one thing I'm good at, it's puttin' a bullet in the right spot when the need arises."

"Sweet Jesus," Ray muttered. "I knew damn well I shoulda pulled stakes an' headed fer Mexico last month. Somethin' told me things was about to turn sour."

Slocum ignored Ray completely now. All his attention was on Barlow. If Ray took off, he would be easy enough to track down, after the shoot-out with Barlow was finished. Slocum didn't want to shoot Ray. Killing an unarmed man had never been his way of doing things.

Slocum carried his rifle in his left hand with the muzzle pointed at the sun. Until Barlow made a threatening move, Slocum would show no signs of looking for trouble.

When the distance between them had closed to less than two hundred yards, Barlow reined to a halt. He studied Slocum and Ray for a moment before he shouted across the distance.

"Let the boy go!" he cried. "I see you got his hands tied!"

Slocum shook his head. "He stays with me all the way to Fort Sill. He's got some talking to do to Major Thompson."

Now it was Barlow's turn to shake his head. "Can't let that happen, stranger. I'm just tellin' you one more time to turn him loose. Otherwise, I'm gonna have to kill you."

Slocum sat stock-still, frozen, muscles tensed for the moment when things started happening. "I'm telling you one last time he stays with me. As to the killin' part, it ain't been decided yet who's gonna die here today."

"You're the sumbitch who's been messin' around with

them Comanches," Barlow shouted. "We don't need no Injun-lovin' sons of bitches 'round here. I'll be doin' every white man in this part of the Territory a favor when I blow you out of that saddle."

"You're mistaken on two counts, Barlow. First is, I ain't no kind of son of a bitch. I resent it on account of my ma and pa. They were good folks, and I'm takin' offense to that remark. Second thing, I'm gonna be a little harder to kill than you think. There's been plenty who've tried. But just to show you I'm a sportin' man, I'll let you make the first move. Bring that rifle down on me or make a grab for your pistol. It don't make a damn bit of difference either way."

"You talk mighty tough. Got one small favor to ask before I kill you. Always did want to know a man's name before I sent him to hell's gates."

Slocum was sure Barlow was only trying to buy time, waiting for him to let down his guard. "Name's John Slocum. They tell me you go by Bob Barlow. That'll be a real easy name to carve into a headstone. The undertaker won't have no trouble with the spelling."

As he had expected, while Slocum was talking, Barlow whipped his rifle to his shoulder. In the same fraction of time, Slocum jerked up his Winchester and fired.

Twin explosions spooked the horses. Slocum's Palouse ducked its head and jumped backward, while the bay carrying the young butcher wheeled and took off at a run.

Startled by the rifle shot, Barlow's horse reared on its hind legs. But Slocum's attention was fixed on Barlow and the way his head jerked back when the bullet struck his left cheekbone.

Barlow toppled out of the saddle. He landed on his back with a grunt, dropping his rifle before he fell. His horse galloped off, trailing its reins.

Slocum turned in the direction of Ray's runaway horse. "I said stop that horse or I'll shoot!" he bellowed.

Ray glanced over his shoulder at Slocum and the rifle he

was pointing at him. He drew back on the bay's reins and brought the animal to a halt. "Don't shoot!" he screamed at the top of his lungs. "I'm comin' back! It was this damn horse that ran away!"

Slocum nodded and heeled his stud in Barlow's direction at a walk, for now there was no hurry. Barlow's left boot had already begun to twitch with death throes.

Slocum stopped when he came to the body. He swung down with his rifle balanced in his palm. A glaze was beginning to form over Barlow's eyes. The gunman's head lay in a spreading pool of blood. A plug of curly black hair lay on the grass near his left ear where Slocum's slug had passed through his skull.

"I warned you I was hard to kill, Mr. Barlow," he said in a quiet, emotionless voice while Ray was riding up. "Now you've got this great big hole in your head, because you wouldn't listen to me. I doubt you can hear me, but if you can, I never did take kindly to being called a son of a bitch, and I take it even harder when a man aims a gun at me. Too bad you won't be around to pass on the lesson you learned today."

"Holy cow," Ray whispered from the back of the bay. "You just shot down Bob Barlow. I never seen nobody as fast as you."

Slocum took a last look at the dying man. "I explained it to you before," he said, turning to mount his Palouse. "Bein' fast ain't all that important, most times. We fired at nearly the same time . . . hell, maybe he even got his shot off first. It didn't go where he wanted it to. Mine did. Now he's layin' in the grass, leakin' blood like a bucket with a hole in it. He'll be dead in a few minutes."

Slocum gathered his reins and mounted the stud. "I want you to take a good look at him," Slocum added as he turned his horse for Fort Sill. "The same thing's gonna happen to you unless you ride right up to Major Thompson's office and tell him everything you know about Bill Anderson's operation."

Ray's face was the color of chalk. "I'll do it, Mr. Slocum, only please don't change your mind an' shoot me anyways. I'll tell that Major everythin'. I won't leave nothin' out."

Barlow made a soft gurgling sound as their horses moved away from the body and the bloodstained grass.

23

Major Bruce Thompson glowered at the bulky man before him. Anderson, in leg irons and handcuffs, was flanked by two uniformed soldiers. Sheriff Wall and a deputy stood nearby guarding Elmer and Ray, who were both wearing wrist manacles. The ranch cook was chained to the others. He lowered his whiskered face as the major addressed the prisoners.

"You're all under arrest for government fraud and cattle theft, and there may be other charges to follow against you, Mr. Anderson. You'll be taken to the guardhouse. Tomorrow morning, you and your associates will be taken by military escort to Fort Smith to appear before Judge Isaac Parker. He'll set a trial date and file formal charges against each of you, depending upon the roles you played in this disgraceful affair."

Ray's chin was quivering. "They call Judge Parker the Hangin' Judge," he said.

Major Thompson shrugged. "You may escape the hangman's rope because you cooperated and gave us a signed confession. That'll be up to Judge Parker." Thompson spoke to the guards. "Take them to the guardhouse. Then inform Captain Carter to mount a detail with a wagon at first light tomorrow. He'll be taking these men to Fort Smith.''

Slocum leaned against the porch post listening to the major until Anderson and the others began to trudge away from headquarters building. He had just turned to untie his horse when a word from the major stopped him.

"Sorry about that Fannie Price woman," he said. "She left town yesterday with a drummer. She told Sheriff Wall to tell you she got tired of waiting."

Slocum grinned. "Women can be impatient creatures. It's all for the best, most likely."

"I want you to know how much the army, and myself, appreciate what you did for us," Thompson continued. "I'm embarrassed that this sort of thing could go on right under our noses. We have George Tatum in a cell. I sent a telegram to Washington informing the Bureau of Indian Affairs about his scheme with Anderson. He'll be facing serious charges himself. While I can't prove it, this may have been his idea all along."

"Maybe now these Indians will get some decent food," Slocum said.

Thompson nodded. "I intend to see to it myself, until the Bureau sends out a new Indian agent. We're handing out rations from our own sutler's supplies, to make sure nothing is spoiled or infested with weevils. We started first thing this morning providing the Indians with food."

Slocum prepared to mount, sticking his left boot in his stirrup. "I'll be heading on up to Denver, Major, after I see some mares near Santa Fe. I was headed that way when all this started. I'm glad you're giving those Indians enough to get them by. And I hope those soldiers who killed and injured the Comanche women are punished."

"The men you pointed out to me are all confined to their quarters until I hold a full investigation. They will be discharged from the army, I can assure you of that. And there may be criminal charges against whoever was responsible for the death of the woman. Again, you have my sincere thanks, Mr. Slocum. I wouldn't have discovered this stolen beef scheme without your help, and the men responsible for these wrongdoings are now certain to be punished . . . sadly, including some of my own soldiers.''

Slocum settled into the saddle. His gear was tied behind the cantle, ready for the trail. "One more thing, Major. How is the Kwahadie girl, Senatey?''

Thompson glanced across the parade ground to the gates. ''I think your answer is waiting for you right there, outside the fort.''

Slocum turned. He saw an Indian girl on a pinto pony and two copper-skinned Comanche men on sorrel horses just beyond the entrance into Fort Sill.

Thompson spoke. "The Comanche named Conas asked to be notified when you got back. He said he had something he wanted to say to you regarding the girl. It appears he brought her with him. I don't recognize the other one.''

''I'll talk to 'em on my way out of town. I'll be seein' you, Major, sometime or another when I get back this way. And good luck. I figure things'll stay peaceful here, so long as those Indians get enough to eat.''

''Best of luck to you, Mr. Slocum. I must say you are a very unusual man. Most men would have ridden past all this difficulty without giving it a moment's thought. For some reason, you stayed and helped us expose a serious case of federal fraud. We are all in your debt.''

Slocum gave the major a lazy salute and turned his horse for the gates.

When he rode up to Conas and Senatey and the other man, an older Indian he had never seen before, Conas gave the sign for peace. Slocum returned it, glancing quickly at Senatey. To his surprise, she was smiling.

Conas began speaking in Comanche. ''You have a brave heart, *Tosi Tivo*. We have food. Our children are no longer crying with hunger. From where the sun now stands, you will be a friend to all *Sata Teichas*.''

''I am grateful. My heart is happy that the children are

not hungry,'' he replied, stumbling over one or two Comanche words that were difficult to say. "I go now, to the land of mountains to the north where I live. *Suvate*.''

Conas inclined his head toward the girl. "Senatey wishes to have words with you alone. She will ride with you until you come to the boundary of this Stinking Place. Her uncle, Quahip, has given his agreement.''

The older Indian closed his fist over his heart.

Senatey heeled her pony to ride beside Slocum as they rode westward toward the setting sun. For several minutes, until they were well away from the fort, she said nothing. Slocum found her silence a bit uncomfortable. She looked at him now and then, but only in sidelong glances.

They left the reservation barracks behind, crossing the hills where a handful of Indian ponies grazed on thin grass, and still Senatey was silent. He wondered if she was embarrassed to talk to a white man who was a virtual stranger. He remembered what he'd been told, that she had a deep hatred for all white men because of what they had done to her people, so it had puzzled him when Conas said that she had words she wanted to say to him in private.

They began a slow descent toward a narrow stream lined with red oak trees. By now, the sun had become an orange ball on the horizon.

"Conas said you had words for me,'' he said in Comanche. Then he recalled that she spoke some English, so he added, "And he said you wanted to say them where no one else would hear.''

She looked down at the pony's mane. Her slender fist was knotted into the hair to help her stay atop the pinto's withers without a saddle. Her face still bore bruises, and in a spot or two, her legs showed purple marks from the beating the soldiers had given her. She was still one of the most beautiful women he'd ever set eyes on, and that amounted to a considerable number. "The soldiers who hurt you will be punished. I have the major's word on it,'' he added when no words came from Senatey's lips.

She pointed to the stream and a thick grove of oaks shedding leaves the color of blood. "We talk there. No one see us talk there."

He wondered why she was so concerned about anyone seeing them having a conversation. Yet he said nothing as he turned his Palouse to ride in the direction she pointed.

They rode into the trees, and Senatey immediately dismounted to tie her pony to a low tree limb. Slocum followed her example and stepped down. Dark shadows blanketed the forest floor and the banks of the creek as the sun sunk below the hills.

Senatey still seemed uncertain, perhaps unsure of what she wanted to say. The deerskin dress she wore now was different, a white color with tiny rows of beads around the neckline. She came over to him hesitantly, searching his face. For a time she simply looked at him.

"Are the words hard to say?" he asked, when it seemed her silence lasted too long.

She smiled and averted her gaze. "You not same as other *Tosi Tivo*. You have good heart. I want say this. You take me to white medicine man. I no want to go. White medicine man have good heart also. I say bad words to you and to white medicine man. I was afraid. I was wrong to be afraid of you and white medicine man. All *Tosi Tivo* not same."

"It's okay, Senatey. I understand. We all fear things we think are bad. I'm glad you don't feel that way toward me or Dr. Green now. There are many good white men. Some, as you know, are bad. The color of a man's skin does not make him good or bad. It's what is in his heart that counts."

She signed that she understood. "You have woman?"

Her question took him completely by surprise. "No, I do not have a woman. I move around an awful lot. It would be hard to have a woman when I'm gone so much of the time."

She was still avoiding his eyes. "Quahip say I can be

your woman, if you want woman. If soldier chief let me go with you.''

Slocum wasn't quite sure what to say. "Tell Quahip I'm real grateful. If I wanted a woman, it would be you. You are very pretty. Downright beautiful, in fact. But I've still got some traveling to do. I live in the north country where mountains are tall. It is far away. Maybe if I come back and talk to Major Thompson in two or three moons, he'll let you come with me. But first, I must go home, to the mountains, and I have to go alone. Do you understand?"

She gave the sign. She understood. Yet there was a trace of sorrow behind her eyes.

"It isn't because of you, Senatey. Please make sure that you understand this."

She nodded without looking at him.

He took a chance and reached for her shoulders, very slowly so as not to frighten her. When she felt his touch, she stiffened.

"Don't be afraid," he told her gently. "I only want to give you a white man's kiss. It's our way of showing good feelings toward a woman."

"I have seen *Tosi Tivo* do this," she said. "It is not the way of the *Sata Teichas*."

"I'll only do it if you'll let me. I won't kiss you if you are afraid."

She looked up into his eyes. "I not afraid. I do not know how to do this thing."

"I'll show you," he whispered, thumbing back his hat before he bent down, still holding her shoulders as gently as he knew how.

He let his lips brush against hers. She stood still with a puzzled expression on her face.

"This is called . . . kiss?" she asked.

Slocum smiled. "Sort of. You're supposed to kiss me back by putting your lips against mine. You can leave them there for a spell, if it feels okay."

"Try again," she said softly, pursing her lips the way he'd done his.

He drew her closer, until their bodies were touching, and placed his mouth over hers. He felt her relax in his arms, and she allowed his lips to linger.

Then slowly, she raised her hands and put her arms around his neck, adding more pressure with her mouth. Her breathing came faster, whispering through her tiny nostrils.

They kissed for a very long time, and her embrace gradually tightened around his neck. Then she pulled back to look at him.

"Is good," she said, her arms remaining around him. "Is good," she said again. "Make me feel warm. I do not know right words."

"Those words are plenty good enough," he assured her, as the dusk deepened into darkness around them. "Sometimes, a man and a woman lie down in the grass to kiss. I can put my arms around you real gently and hold you close to me."

"Show me this," she said. "I will lie down with you. You put arms around me. Kiss again."

He reached for one of her hands and led her over to the stream where the grass was thick. Kneeling down first, he pulled her down beside him. Then he lay on his side, and Senatey lay next to him. Slocum put one arm behind her and placed his palm in the small of her back.

"This is better," he said, tossing his hat to the ground, admiring the perfect lines of her face. He couldn't help but notice that her nipples had turned hard underneath her dress and its hem had risen higher to reveal more of her legs.

He kissed her, and she returned his kiss, putting her hand on his right cheek and stroking it gently. Her lips were warm and sweet, and as he kissed her he wondered if riding away from the lovely Comanche maiden might be one of the biggest mistakes of his life.